I just want to thank all you beautiful souls. Thank you for all the support and feedback.

Thank you again and stay forever blessed.

Les Be Honest... I'm so quick to tell the male partners during my nymphomaniac journey, but there are two sides...I mean, I did have the best of both worlds while it lasted.

Les•Be•HONEST

The Beginning

I FOUND MYSELF ALWAYS trying to *find myself*. Growing up, I was a very confused girl, but I knew too much. Let me make this make sense, I was *confused* on why I was *confused*, I've never seen my mom with a woman that wasn't family. I knew it was *wrong* to have feelings for someone of the same sex. So why was I *so attracted* to women? I would go to church to pray the demons out, I questioned God on why I liked to hunch girls in my head *(like all the time)* ... I heard no voice in return, though.

I would even talk to my counselor about the way girls made me feel and he told me I *would grow out of it*; it didn't mean anything. I couldn't shake this *'homosexual demon' – not even in the church house.* I remember this day like it was yesterday. In the middle of the church service, I left the altar to go use the restroom. I quietly got up, holding my index finger up until I was no longer visible. I knocked on the door because it was shut. I heard nothing, so I proceeded to go in and to my surprise, there she was... dressing. She was *beautiful*. She was seven years older than me, light-skinned, big titties, a nice fat ass, and some dick-sucking lips.

"I'm sorry, I didn't hear you say you were in here. I'll come back," I said.

She replied, *"I didn't say anything because I caught onto your voice, you can come on in."*

I was shocked. I didn't know what to do, so I walked on in–like she requested. She slowly started unbuttoning the top buttons of her shirt, I couldn't bring my eyes to look anywhere else.

"Why are you looking down, little girl?" She asked, as she walked towards me.

I began backing up as she moved forward, until there was nowhere else to go. My back was up against the restroom door (*which happened to be red... if you didn't catch that, it means you haven't read my book 'The Red Room,' and you need to grab that ASAP*). She looked me in my eyes, grabbed my hands to place them onto her breast. She kissed me on my lips and smiled. I was nervous, so I did nothing. She pulled her titties out of her bra – I wanted to suck her nipples, but I was too nervous–I forgot I had to pee. I didn't even say anything to her, I think *that* freaked her out. She waited for me to do something or at least say something, and I never did. However, I was *lowkey* mad when she put them pretty motherfuckas up.

After that, she never spoke to me. She even went so far as calling me and my little sisters *'ugly'* because we were not *light skinned*, like her and my older sister. I didn't let that bother me because...*I know what happened in that restroom, last Sunday.*

I did not understand why I was an *automatic sex magnet.* I have always been fascinated with a woman's body, but these motherfuckas were raping me on the cool – with my consent, it was still out of order, *considering the years.* The girls were sometimes *worse* than the boys. I began staying inside the house, just looking at magazines – due to the girl down the street from my grandmother's house, who went from grabbing me by the coochie, to sticking her tongue down my throat, to waiting/wanting to eat my pussy. My fucked-up ass *liked* it, but she wanted to do that *every day,* and it wasn't fun anymore... *It was the thrill for me, though.*

My mom had a sorry ass nigga that would come fight her on the job, so she ended up leaving Home Health for a while. We moved to the projects for a few months so my mom could stack [money]. It was also closer to her job, and the school I had to go to, since I had been kicked out of Alamo Elementary.

We (*my sisters and I*) made friends with the kids in the neighborhood. Automatically, the 'born gay,' bi-curious ones, and lesbians wanted to be friends. I befriended them because I knew 3 out of 5 would want to eat my pussy. *I shit you not*, a week after we moved in, one of my sister's friends wanted to play *'house.'* She wanted me to play the *mama* and she was going to be the *daddy*. Of course, we had no kids, *so we had to make some*. She wanted me to hunch her and let her eat my coochie. When she went down to eat my coochie, she licked the top of it. It wasn't like the girl in the country, but she was younger than her, as well.

There was another girl in the projects that stayed up the street. She was a sophomore in high school, a Pentecostal church girl, but the type that would *rebel* and grow out of the *'girl'* people wanted her to be–and ultimately, become a stud. She is the niece of my mom's husband. I knew she liked girls; it was no secret. One night, she came over and after my sisters and mother fell asleep, she asked me to play a game.

"Have you ever played truth or dare?" She asked.

"No, I've never played that," I replied.

She said, *"It's easy! All you have to do is pick 'truth' or 'dare' when I ask you, truth or dare."*

"Okay," I quickly replied, anxious to start the got damn game already.

"Truth or dare?" She asked.

"Truth," I answered.

She wasted no time, she asked, *"Is it true that you like girls?"*

Gay people know gay people... I couldn't lie. She already knew the answer, but I told her anyway.

"Yes, I like girls." I started to ask her, *"Bitch, do you?"* But, following the rules, I asked her, *"Truth or dare?"*

"Dare!" She said, like a daredevil.

(I was scared to dare her to do anything, I didn't know if she would be up for my dare.)

"I'm scared to dare you, you pick your dare," I told her.

"You sure you want me to pick?" She asked, before telling me, *"you might not be ready for that."*

We went back and forth, until I read her mind. Giving into her thoughts, I said, *"I dare you to let me suck your titties."*

That's not what she wanted, but I had to start slow. She reached behind her back and unsnapped her bra with two fingers... *She had some nice titties.*

Once she fully removed her bra, she grabbed me, placing me on top of her. I started rotating my hips while leaning down to get to them *chocolate nipples.* I started with the left nipple, working my way to the right one. She grabbed her titties, holding them together so I could put my face into them.

"Slow down before you cum," she said. I knew what she was saying, but I didn't know *what she meant.* My body started to shake, that's when she said, *"Get up, let me show you something."* She slid her pajamas off and told me to take off my shorts, I complied. She then went under my shirt, and cupped my titties before sucking them, laying me back before getting on top of me. *"Open your legs, I'ma show you something then I want you to try it on me."* When I opened my legs, she placed her

left leg above my right outer thigh and her right leg in between my left thigh and started grinding. Back then the '*tick*' was the dance move, she started *ticking* in circles like she was from the islands. *"Now do that to me,"* she ordered.

"I'll try," I replied.

I got on top of her and did exactly what she did in the beginning. But, once I got the hang of it, *I switched it up on her ass*. Back-and-forth like a swing, deep circles like a merry-go-round, and ticking like a clock... put that shit together—that, my friends, is how you start a *hurricane*.

She said, *"Get yo freaky ass up, yo ass not about to have me sprung."*

"You started it, I was just doing what you asked," I told her.

"I dare you to let me eat your pussy," she suggested. She wanted to do that a whole hour ago... when I read her mind.

"Okay, but don't hurt me," I said to her.

"Trust me, I won't! It will feel good," she assured me. I don't even know why I said that... It wasn't like that was the first time. I was nervous as hell, I moaned soon as her tongue landed on me. *"You gotta be quiet or I'ma stop."*

I placed my hands over my mouth, and she continued. This wasn't the forced, *twisted shit* I was used to, or into. It was way more passionate than that; I felt her tongue-twisting *inside* of me, in-and-out... fast, then real slow, then she would go faster. Then, she took her tongue out of my pussy and kissed my ass cheek. She started licking my pussy—up and down—then flicking her tongue on my clit. I pushed her head off me and told her I couldn't take anymore, she tried to eat some more, but I *seriously couldn't handle it anymore*.

"What's wrong? You didn't like it?" She asked.

"It felt too good, I couldn't stop shaking," I said, still shaking.

With me saying that, she eased up, but she wasn't quite finished. She wanted to play in the cream and wetness. That is when she told me, *"You're really blessed... you got some good. When you get older, what's between your legs will be worth more than gold."*

That night was the beginning of something that lasted *over a year...* through her many relationships, and some more shit. AOL was big back then, and she had the internet, so I would log in on her computer while she talked to her girlfriends and internet lovers.

I was young but when I tell you, I had *too much sense* for the average adult. I talked like I created this flat world, and every species in it! I was logged in online at her house, catching up on IM's (*instant messages*), while floating from chatroom to chatroom. She came into her room crying, because she and her long-distance girlfriend broke up after an argument.

She walked over to the computer where I was sitting and put her hand in my shirt, lightly pinching and rolling my nipples. I took my jacket off so she could get a better feel. I'm watching her undress the rest of me with her eyes from the mirror's view. She noticed me looking and gave me this, *'I'm hungry'* look. I stood up and took off my capris as she pulled my shirt over my head.

As I sat back down in the chair, she massaged my shoulders, back, and my feet. I heard *"You've got mail!"* I looked up to check my mail. I felt my legs spread, but I wasn't expecting *Lalaloopsy* licks in between my legs. I felt her soft tongue on my pussy, so I moved to the edge of the chair, allowing her to stick her tongue *deep* inside of me. She reached up, grabbed my titties, and rocked me *back and forth.*

"Put that little pussy on my face," she said. My toes started throwing up gang signs, I grabbed her head and made her stop. *"Please don't do that, I'm lonely and horny."*

"Ooo..." is all I got out. She cut me off, not with words, but she stuck a finger inside of me... that left me saying sweet nothings–cause I wasn't saying a damn thing that made sense.

"You like that, don't you?" She asked. All I could do was shake my head. I guess I should have opened my mouth and at least tried to say 'yes,' because she followed, *"Oh, you don't like it? Let me try something I saw on this porno."* She gently nibbled on my pussy. She started at the hood of my pussy, working her way to the clit. I started to shake like I was possessed, so, of course, I made her stop. *"I was just getting to the best part!"*

"I'm scared of what will happen next," I replied.

"I want you to cum in my mouth," she said.

"Eww that's nasty... and I don't even know how to cum," I said, trying to end the conversation.

"Just let it flow, don't fight it. You gotta learn to relax... maybe next time."

I told myself there wouldn't be a *'next time.'* I started to feel bad for fucking with her; for one, she was now *family by marriage.* To keep going, she was several years older than me. She began to steal clothes for me, give me money, braid my hair, etc. I started feeling like she was trying to *buy me*, or she felt she owned me. *I even woke up to her eating my pussy one morning!*

"It's 6 AM, granny just caught the bus to work," she said, as I was opening my eyes. I grabbed her by her braids and pushed her face in my pussy. It started feeling good and I accidentally locked my thighs around her

head. I apologized because that was crazy, and I know I scared the both of us. But she didn't mind she said, *"You about to cum, just concentrate."*

I released her head, *I couldn't focus to save my life*, I just think entirely too much. She came and snuggled up behind me. She felt up on me to the point I had to turn around. Since she wasn't going to let me go back to sleep, I rolled over on top of her. I was just going to lay on her to force her to stop, so I could nap just a little longer. She kissed me and rolled me over, trading places. Then, she rubbed her finger against my pussy to see how wet it was. (*Just so we're clear if there's possible action, I'ma always be wetty, I mean ready lol*)

After seeing that I was wet, she wiggled her finger around until it was inside of me, then laid on it, making it like she had a penis – and fucked me! That was a little *too wild* for me. I think at that moment, she *really* thought she was a boy or had a *penis*, however you wanna say it. I won't lie, it felt good, but she made me want to explore sex further... *with a male*. I laid there, motionless, but my thoughts were roaming my mind 125 miles per hour.

When we finished, I told myself, *"Yeah, I'm not doing this with her anymore."* I said that shit and stuck to it. I would still go over there to chill from time to time, but that extra shit was dead for me. I cut her off for good a year later. School just ended for the summer, we no longer stayed on the eastside, but I was *overjoyed* when we got to visit.

I went to catch up with my old friends and I saw her. She asked me if I wanted to go to the mall with her. I didn't even ask to leave with her–I just left, and it was instant karma, this girl went in there stealing them people's stuff. The bitch lied and told them people that the clothes were for me and her. But, when they saw the size of the pants, they could determine–for a fact–that I couldn't fit *shit* inside that bag.

She put the thought into my head to explore sex *deeper*, but I just couldn't find a boy to like. *I hated them*! The only dude I wanted was Fred, I fell in love with him in 4th grade.

The school year was back in session–my first semester of 7th grade.

Nervous as any other kid in the building, I went in trying to be as normal as possible. But it was *so many bitches that I wanted to fuck*. It was a few white girls at McNeil (Jr High) that was *stacked*, I can't even lie. There were maybe 100 blacks [students] total–that's both 7th & 8th grade *combined*. I became friends with a white girl named Shayla, I liked her cause she talked her shit, everybody else feared me... however, she didn't. She wanted to be black *so* bad, but she never overstepped those boundaries of knowing she wasn't.

The first semester, we kicked it tough; after school, on the phone, at the school dances, she even left one of the dances with me after they [school administration] realized I was not supposed to be there. We hung so tough; our parents wanted to meet each other. After the parents met the first time, I got to go over to her house. It was different from the household I was used to... *and yes it was because they are white*. She had no chores, for one. She could cuss, and when she wasted some chips on the floor, I told her to sweep it up, this bitch said, *"That's a mom's job, I don't know how to sweep. Just leave it on the floor for the dogs or for my mom to get up."* I knew then that I would never have a white lover.

I grabbed the broom and swept it up, she was shocked I knew how to clean. I told her, *"Sweeping ain't cleaning."*

That night, we danced until it was time for the *real* dance. No one knew I had rhythm, it shocked them when I did the 'lean back' with them. I heard a group of girls say, *"Omg, I didn't know she could dance!"*

A school full of white girls thought *my colored ass could not dance*!? What the fuck is wrong with them? I laughed because that was not even *dancing*. Nazia, Sara, and I were the only three black girls there that night, but along with Shiloh and Shayla, we formed a dance circle. I let everybody go first because I wanted everyone to shine before I killed shit. We drew attention like a muthafucka... before we knew it, we were the center of attention, but that wasn't stopping shit! They went crazy when I started popping, (it wasn't called '*twerking*' back then).

"*How do you pop with your hands straight?*" Shiloh asked.

"*I have to turn my hands inward to do that,*" Shayla added.

I showed them a few dance moves before the night ended. Shayla's stepdad dropped me off at home, and we had made plans to have a sleepover at my house the next weekend.

Next weekend came, Shayla got dropped off and the party began. One of my older sisters' friends was there that attended McNeil as well, so we danced, played truth, or dare (*what a classic game*) on the trampoline, ordered a pizza combo, and watched scary movies while constantly apologizing for the smell of my mother's *marijuana*. I swear my room was *haunted* (*got facts to prove the whole house was haunted*), so I never slept in there.

I only went to my room to get dressed and write. I moved my bed into my sisters' room, so we didn't have to lay four to a bed. It was time for bed, shower, and relaxing. This girl came out of the bathroom *differently!* Her straight hair was curly, her blue eyes were now brown, her skin was ghostly... ass still fat and she was still cute *without* her make-up.

We talked until she fell asleep, and I laid on my back like I had a stiff dick and prayed to God to take my sick-ass thoughts away. I knew she was sexually active, and she wasn't so much '*bi*', she was more of a regular freak. Whenever fun presented itself, she was front and center. When my thoughts shifted, I laid there laughing at myself, thinking, *"What if this bitch leaves her hair all on my pillow, like a cat."*

Finally, I got to a place where I was dozing off, and just when I got there, her hand slid across my chest like she wanted to hold me, but I was laying on my back. I pushed her off me, pushing her up against the wall. I tried to fall asleep again and about twenty minutes later, she was back next to me. I was moving her again, shit, *she was extra dead weight*, which made me believe she was pretending to be asleep. She was my friend; I wasn't going to touch her–asleep or woke... I couldn't see myself doing that shit. She started to toss and turn, so I turned to my side, but when I woke up through the night, she was cuddled up behind me with her hand around my stomach. I told myself I was going to punch the shit out of her because I know people don't sleep that damn bad. I turned around to push her off me and this bitch was looking me right in my fucking face. She scared the fuck out of me, she started laughing but I didn't get the joke. We didn't talk as much after that... that was simply weird as fuck to me.

In the 8th grade year, we started back talking about the strength she was dating Dustin; (*Dustin was my close friend*). Shayla and I didn't have any classes together that school year, but I met this chick named April. She reminded me of Shayla, but she was black and not as cute in the face, but she was stacked like a grown-ass woman and mean than a bitch. *I love mean girls*; they usually have a deep story on why they are the way they are. We instantly clicked–her boyfriend is one of my brother's best friends... he's a brother to us and *she's Fred's cousin*. One day when April went to the restroom, I went to place our spiral we shared to write notes back and forth and I saw she had another composition book. I honestly thought she had started a spiral with another muthafucka, but it turned out to be her diary. I know I should have minded my own business once I saw it was her diary... but man was it some *juicy* shit in there. She didn't catch me, but once I read what was in there, I had questions, and *I needed answers*!

The next time we swapped the spiral I asked her, "*So you had an abortion?*"

Like we were fifteen and fourteen, *what the fuck*?! She stopped talking to me for a few months until she decided to fucking run away. I told her she could come to stay with me, without asking my mom. We were walking on the eastside one day and ended up running into my mother and her mom's cousin. I'm the only person that knew she had planned on not going home. We walked our way back to my aunt's house where we both were staying for the night. She started to tell me all about her past, parents, and the whole fucked up family until we dozed off. Going to sleep was hard, I felt like something was going to happen, but she wasn't even cute to me. She didn't turn me on, not even a little bit, but lying next to her, I thought about my mom's ex-husband's niece that still stayed up the street with 'granny.' I wanted to leave April in that bed and go sleep with 'her,' I wanted my pussy ate and the more I thought about it, the wetter I got.

She slept wild! She brushed up against me and I pushed her off because her hands were landing directly on my private areas. April's mom searched the eastside when she didn't go home that day, and her cousin that was with my mom informed her that April was safe, and she knew where she was but to wait until the morning to come to pick her up. She didn't want April's mother to pick her up the same night because she probably would have killed her. I woke up to her telling me to move over, she braided my hair that night and my hair, wrapped up, found its way under my body. Her mom pulled up ten minutes later and we didn't talk for a while after that. A month later, one of her cousins came to school and told me how April said I was *'pretending'* to be asleep when she felt me touching on her. I was pissed because I wasn't even gone tell nobody about the shit, I really let it go. I read things that could destroy her – *and she was going around saying shit like that...!*

I never confronted her about the situation because she never brought it to me and she knew I would read her, her Muthafuckin rights! I made sure from that point on, I would only be around her in front of people and when we had to sleep next to one another, I slept at the opposite end.

The summer was nothing but fights–but the more I hung with April, *the more I saw Fred*. I finally gave up on Fred, due to him moving to North Carolina... *that shit broke my heart*. I started trying to find myself again but this time, I just wanted to be left alone.

I started hanging with my mom's old boyfriend's nieces. One of them (*Lani*) would be going to Hirschi [High School] with me the following month. The other two sisters (*'Pear' and Jo'*) would be riding the bus, like me. Lani hung with this girl named *Nyla* and when I saw her, (Nyla) I automatically knew she was gay. However, I was unsure of how to get her attention – *hell, I didn't even know her*. But anyways, Lani's mom was dating this man that lived across the street from Hirschi. An elderly man, raising all his grandkids. One of them happened to be deaf, but she was gay as well. I *always* noticed her staring at me, and one day, I did basic signing [sign language] with her, trying to see what the fuck was the deal. She was trying to tell me by mouth [with no voice] that she wanted to eat my pussy... *I don't even think ya'll know how scary that sounds*. Another time I was over there, I went in to use the restroom and she walked in on me. As I was wiping myself, she got on her knees, motioning for me to put my pussy on her mouth... begging, "*Please.*"

I started to beat her ass, but I screamed instead! I'm not being rude because she was deaf, *she was an ugly girl!* It's really fucked up, because she's the type of *ugly* that got treated badly–just because she was ugly.

It was time for Freshman year... I wanted to start clean, I was still a virgin–and I wasn't sure if I was still into girls. I told myself I would never find anybody worth being in a relationship with. Lani and I started the first day of school together. She called me the night before and told me to wear my jean jacket and some burgundy pants. She also insisted after I caught the bus, to meet her at her mom's boyfriend's place so we could walk in together. We walked in together, but after that day, we drifted apart.

The same day, I went to history class and saw Nyla, sitting on the right side of the classroom in the first row... just five seats back. I immediately went to the left side of the room. A month had gone by, and I hadn't talked to Lani, but we spoke when passing. However, Lani and Nyla fell out and Nyla ended up beating up Lani. Nyla and I slowly started talking about strength–we were partners for an electoral assignment. I went to Pear and Jo's house that day after school and they asked me to spend the night. Their mom worked overnights, so they could do whatever they wanted. They had made plans to invite Stuart (*may he rest in peace*), and a dude named Deon over. They told me I could invite someone if I wanted to. I helped them set up for the night even though I wasn't going to stay–because I just wasn't with it, but I assured them we could have an '*all-girls night*' the following day, because I wanted to hear all about how their night went.

We met at the playground at noon to discuss the plans for the night. Pear said she had some weed, and Jo' said she had some drank. I listened without agreeing to anything other than showing up. 10 o'clock hit – that was the time we had agreed to be walking out the door so we could all link up at once, since it was dark outside. I saw Pear walking with two white girls (*Amanda and Melissa*), so I hurried to meet them. The night started cool, we were all sitting around just talking and having fun. Amanda and Melissa ended up leaving, I walked them home with Pear, so she could smoke on the way back.

"I can't wait to tell you what happened last night," Pear said.

"Why didn't you just tell me in there?" I asked.

She answered, *"Because he used to mess with my sister..."*

I didn't say anything after that–I was shocked. When we got back to the apartment, we went into her room and started talking. Pear told me about Stuart putting fire to her nipple, and how she sucked his dick... she even went into details about how *big* it was. I wasn't interested in hearing about it, because I had a huge crush on his cousin, *Darin*, back in the day. Darin and I called ourselves 'dating,' but he broke up with me the first time – because *Stuart was in love with me.* Jo busted into the room and asked if we wanted to play a game of *'Truth or Dare.'* I wanted to play, but it seemed like every time I played that game, motherfuckas loved expressing how they like the same sex... it was becoming too predictable – *"but what the hell,"* I thought, and played anyways.

Jo' asked, *"Who wants to go first?"*

"Truth or dare?" Pear asked.

"Truth," I replied.

"Is it true you liked a girl before?" Pear asked me.

"Fuck no!" I said, in a tone that made both girls look upside my head.

"Jo, truth or dare?" I asked her.

She quickly answered, *"Ima have to go with truth."*

"Is it true that you tried to talk to Darin?" I asked her.

I only asked her because when Darin and I broke up the second time, I heard they were in the park–*trying to sing duets and shit*!

"Omg, why would you ask me that?" Jo replied, answering my question with a question.

"Girl, you already answered my question, don't worry about it," I said.

"Pear, truth or dare?" I asked.

"Dare, cause ya'll scary, and it's just a game," she replied.

"I dare you to slap the fuck out of your sister! I'm joking! I dare you to take a shot." I said, laughing.

She took a shot, followed by a shot for me, and said, *"Stop with the boring shit, let's get crunk!"*

"Have you ever sucked dick?" Pear asked me.

"Well, hell no! You know I haven't," I remarked with disgust.

"It's not bad... it's just skin. Stop being scary!" Jo' said.

That's when Jo' told us about how she sucked Deon's dick the night before. *(And before a muthafucka tries to put this shit together, I'm not talking about Darin's brother, Deon!)* But as she told the story, it sounded more forced than by nature, but I didn't cut her off.

"I was scared for it being my first time, but all day, Deon kept telling me to drink water so my mouth wouldn't reject his dick. He came and picked me up. We went to his apartment, and I sucked his dick, like I saw in this porn. I pulled his skin back and sucked the mushroom-looking part and slid myself down the rest of it. I tried to put it all in my mouth... I heard you could feel dick in your throat," Jo' said.

"Ooooooo, that ain't nothing! I remember I was sucking Stuart's big fat dick, and almost threw up, and that muthafucka had the nerve to tell me

I better not stop, or he was going to find somebody else to do it..." Pear said, ending Jo's story.

"*Well, I'm sorry I don't have any dick-sucking stories too–*" I said before Pear cut me off.

She said, "*Lissa, you gotta be gay, I don't even think you like niggas! Everybody knows, I like niggas and bitches,*" Pear said nonchalantly, while shrugging her shoulders.

"*Have you ever kissed a guy–or seen a dick, up close in person?*" Jo' asked.

These hoes were really judging me because I had no dick-sucking stories. I was ready to fight on the cool, but I still considered them *family*, even though my mom was no longer with their uncle. I eased up and decided to open up, because if I'm being honest, I'm hard to figure out... you'll *only* know if I don't care if it's *known*.

"*Well... Got damn! No, I'm not gay! I've been eaten out by a girl before. I do like niggas; I just don't think they're attracted to me. I've kissed guys, and I've seen two dicks before. And before you bitches ask me why I said, 'I didn't like girls,' let me explain. I'm only attracted to the physical, I could never see myself falling in love with a girl or woman,*" I explained.

"*Damn, did you wanna take that to the grave or something?*" Pear asked me.

We all just laughed. We started talking about school and how shit was going. Pear is older than me, but she failed a grade, so she was in junior high. Jo' and I were in high school. We were both freshmen, but she was supposed to be a grade up from me. I loved hearing about how Rider's football team was doing, and they *loved* hearing about the black boys at Hirschi. Conversation started to make us tired. Jo' called over Deon, so I was going to bunk with Pear.

Pear and I started talking about the things we couldn't say around her sister, and this bitch looked at me and said, *"I wanna ask you something... I'm serious."*

I already knew she was going to ask me something *gay-related.* In my mind, I knew I wasn't going to be able to stay after whatever was going to happen next.

"What's up?" I asked.

"I think you should let me eat you out," Pear insisted.

"I'm not even about to play like that with you," I replied.

I laid there on her deer-hunting comforter, and the longer I laid there, the madder she made me. Five minutes felt like two hours, I wanted to cuss her out, but I got my bitch-ass up, and hit that sidewalk and took my ass home. It wasn't a long walk, but since people had been out breaking into cars bad, a curfew was in effect – and I didn't want to be caught up in either scenario.

"Why are you banging on this door at damn near 2 o'clock in the morning Renee'?!" Nikki asked.

"Cause, she gay and I felt uncomfortable," I said.

"Whhoooooo?!! Which one?!" She screamed.

"The little sister," I replied, keeping it short.

My fucking brain was fried at that point. I called Darin just to have somebody to talk to. He laughed and called me 'gay' the entire time.

I think I was super pissed because she reminded me of a 'Grindylow' (*google it*) – scary in the face... like, for real! I wasn't going to say shit else about it, but after that day, she started talking about me to Melissa and Amanda – *Melissa didn't even know me.* I met her a few nights ago, but Pear talked about me so bad, Melissa came and knocked on my door and ran [told] me *everything* she said. Amanda was the second person to tell me. She had to wait until her dad left, *because he hated too many black people in his house at once* – Hahahahaha no bullshit!

Anyways, Amanda had reported the same shit Melissa said *(I don't move off no 'he said–she said' shit).*

I instructed both of them, *"If she said that when I walk around here, and she speaks to you, call that bitch out on her bullshit, or don't bring me back shit else!"*

We walked around the corner and down to the front to check the mail. On the way back, Pear was inside this lady's house–but popped her head out to say, *"Hey bitches!"* Being all friendly and shit...

"Don't speak, if you was talking shit, my nigga," I remarked.

"Girl, nobody was talking about you! And I hope them whites' bitches ain't say that cause I'll beat they ass now!" Pear exclaimed.

"Bitch you ain't gone beat my ass! Don't think just because I'm white, I can't fight, or I'm scared!" Amanda clapped back.

Melissa chimed in, *"Bitch, you WAS talking shit about her, and I'm not scared, so what's up...?"*

Amanda ran in on her, *it was drama for three days straight!* Pear told Jo' she was almost jumped and some more crazy shit. Melissa ended up beating Jo's ass.

Amanda's father told her we couldn't be friends anymore. It was just me now, and I think Pear and Jo' thought Melissa and Amanda were needing help, because the next day, they both started picking with me.

I talked my shit back... long as a motherfuckas wasn't in my face and in my space, a motherfuckas can talk until they blue in the face.

Pear had been getting her ass beat all fucking week, and I guess she hadn't had enough. I'm minding the business that pays me when Kayla said, *"Girl you know I'll whoop you again."* I start laughing–like I always do. The bus is getting ready to stop at Barwise [Jr. HS]. Kayla said, *"Lissa, she said you was scared of her, that's why you quiet on the bus."*

I forgot what the fuck I said, but I was trying to correct myself. Not because I was scared, but because it was an honest mistake. I was going to talk my shit, but I wanted to talk it *right*. So much for the correction... I heard Pear stomping from the back of the bus, so I turned to get up.

Pear is in my face now, screaming, *"Bitch no I didn't, no I didn't!"*

"Bitch I was trying to correct myself, but you marched up here like you wanna fight," I said.

"Like I said bitch, no I didn't," Pear replied.

She was talking so hard, that spit was flying from her mouth–and onto me–I fucking lost it on her. I upper cut that bitch and she pulled my hair, so I choked her and banged her head on the window. That's when she punched me in the stomach, and I walked on that bitch like I was getting paid to fight. I wanted to knock her fucking face-off! That's when Jo came and broke it up. Kayla came running down the bus saying, *"Y'all better not jump her, I know that!"*

Once they got me off of Pear, they helped her get her books and folders so she could get the fuck off the bus. This bitch waited until she was on the top step to get off of the bus to look back and say, *"Nana-nana, boo-boo..."* – *like she whooped me.* I yanked that bitch down by her crochets and kicked her *off* and *out* of the bus. I told myself I was going to beat her ass again after school because I had a class with Nyla, *and now my hair was a mess!*

I got to school and, of course, it [fight] was all around the school. After the first period, it was time for history class, and I didn't want to go – due to the fact, Nyla would be there as well. I walked in and Nyla had a blue brush on her desk, I asked her to use her brush, and she said *yes...*

Nyla

WHEN I FIRST SAW HER, I knew she was gay [even though she had a boyfriend... that shit was just a cover up]. *Nyla* is the lightest–black person I've seen – to not be mixed with anything. A beautiful individual: she had long beautiful hair, big eyes that fit her, braces on her teeth, and could dress her ass off. She never "overdid" the 'tomboy' shit, but she killed 98 percent of the male's shoe game.

She was an athlete, so she normally hung with her teammates–however, we were becoming friends rather quickly. We started a spiral together (like a notebook that you shared notes with your best friends) just to get to know one another and to keep up, since our schedules were so different.

In our History class, it was natural for us to be partners on projects and reports, since we were friends. We didn't live in the same area, so, during our [30 minute] lunch, we worked on the electoral debate. It was time for a change, he could be the only president with color I'd live to see. *(Kamala Harris isn't black, so please don't start with the bullshit!).* *Nyla* and I were both for Barack Obama-but with two totally different views.

She was "for him" simply because he was black, and I *hated that*. First of all, he's not black; having a *spec* of something in your ethnic background doesn't make up a person's *whole* ethnicity. I wanted to dig deeper – and really present something to Coach Carr, 'ole *red hot ass*! I say that because he's the 'typical white man:' *loves black women but has some 'white power' ways.*

In the middle of her disagreeing with me, I noticed how pretty her lips were.

"Bro, is you listening to me?" She asked.

"I hear you, but what I'm saying is: we need a powerful opening statement. 'My president is black' ain't gone cut it, even though he's going to win," I replied.

Going back to admiring her beauty, I wanted to kiss her. I *really* wanted to climb on the table, place my pussy in front of her, and watch her eat it. I wanted to see her naked. I was *bugging*!

The next day, we had to present our debate to the class. It was also my turn to hand-off the spiral. However, I didn't write her back, so she was *so heated (you would have thought I wrote, 'I hope your mama dies,' or something)*. She had plenty of friends and stayed passing notes with others–I wasn't going to flood her with more *'fan mail.'*

Bro, she was getting *dicked* down–I didn't want to hear that! Coming to school acting like she was pregnant... knowing damn well that he was a cover up... and that I liked her. We were both mad at each other for some shit that we wouldn't speak on, but we still grew into best friends... for the time being anyway...

There was always tension among us, then most days, I wanted to throw her against the wall and *fuck* her. I had the *wildest* dream one night–it almost depict the current situation at hand:

She invited me over to visit after school–or on the weekend and told me that I should come see her play sometime. My dream was more of what would happen if I decided to take her up on her offer.

* In my dream [above], it was a Thursday. However, it was on Friday night when I *had* the dream. We were texting and she invited me over for the weekend, she stayed with her grandparents in Lynwood.

Nyla: *You can spend the night, or you can just come over. Whatever you wanna do, my people don't be trippin'.*

Me: *Did you ask? I'm not tryna get cussed out for being there.*

Nyla: *Are you tryna get yo' pussy ate and played with?*

Me: *Put a finger in it while you eat it. I'm coming over, I'll be there within the hour.*

Nyla: *Bro, don't tell me how to eat pussy, I promise all I need you to do is bring yo' body.*

I arrived within the hour, like I *said* I would. She answered the door wearing a white t-shirt, black Nike shorts, and white low-cut Nike socks. I noticed she had her hair pulled back in a ponytail... her nipples were hard–she had on a sport bra like *all* dykes lol (*she going to cuss me out*).

I pulled the screen door back so I could pass her while pressing up against her at the same time – just to feel her skin. In doing that action, my hand *touched* her pussy. I didn't apologize, but I did move out the way so that she could guide me. We walked through the den, making our way to the living room so that I could speak and introduce myself before we entered the grand-daughter's room to get *nasty and naughty*.

Making my way to her room, I was *immediately* turned on; it was like stepping through a *portal*. Dull blue – gray, white, or yellow if you're a *tetrachromat*. She had these big, black body-pillows that covered her king-size bed. I ran and jumped into her bed while she closed the door behind us. I sat up as she made her way to me, placing my legs around her. I was nervous, but I grabbed her chin and kissed her–like I'd been wanting to do since I first laid eyes on her. She kissed me back, leaning down, causing me to lean with her, until she was on top of me... chest to chest.

"Take off yo' shoes and get up there," Nyla instructed, motioning me to move *up* in the bed.

"You take 'em off... and rub my feet while you at it," I replied. She looked at me crazy, and then leaned down to take my shoes off... but it was too late then.

I wanted to give her a reason to look at me even crazier. I lifted my legs past her head, bringing them a foot passed and above my head, taking my own shoes off. She didn't give a damn that I was flexible (or so I thought), she looked right at my pussy. She grabbed my pussy with two fingers – literally *making* them lips! She kissed the lips she made, getting me wet through my sweats.

"You might as well take them off," she said.

"Why you say that?"

"You know damn well that pussy wet and I wanna see it."

"Okay, Pimp C!" I said while taking off my clothes.

I decided to lose the shirt, so she could see my gold-striped *Victoria's Secret*. I turned to crawl up in the middle of her bed, exposing my thong. She proceeded to smacking my ass, causing me to move faster. As soon as I got under the cover, she wanted me to come to her.

"Come here real quick."

"No, you come here."

"Man, come here, Earlissa."

I threw the covers back, walked up to her like I was lost, and just stood before her. She looked but didn't say anything. I became body-shy at that moment. I turned to get back in the bed and under the cover – that's when she finally said something.

"Bro, who would have known yo' mean ass had a body like this?!"

"I'm not mean..."

"Turn around for a second."

I turned around, asking no questions. She kissed the back of my neck, down to the middle of my back, grabbing me by my waist, while falling back onto the bed. She held me, groping my breast, turning me on. I sat there with my eyes and neck *rolling*.

Nyla, deep massaging my shoulders, made me sink deeper in between her legs. I rubbed her legs, enjoying how she was relaxing me. I'd never felt the energy she had gave off, I could have fell asleep–but that's not what I came here for.

I stood up, grabbing her hand, leading her to her bed like it was mine. I told her to come lay down with me.

Nyla feared what she had started. As for me, I was *already* in another zone, and I wanted her *all* over me. She got into bed. However, she wasn't close–like I wanted her to be, so I pulled her towards me, making her kiss me. She kissed me, I sucked her lips, bringing her back in for another kiss. Switching it up, I licked her lip and hopped on top of her like I was about to ride her. *Ny* grabbed my ass, making it shake... so I rocked back and forth on her, which was the wrong thing to do, because it was traces of cum on her shorts. *(Cum on anything black-colored, is the wrong thing to do... y'all already know!)*

"Let me get that," Nyla said, jumping out of the bed.

"Okay," I replied, clueless and shit... thinking that she's about to undress.

I felt more air... like I didn't have any cover around me. I looked down and *Nyla* was inches from my pussy. It was like a lion entering his kingdom after a long day of hunting. I didn't want to stop her or make her nervous, so I laid back, waiting until she spoke with her tongue–damn near making *me* speak in tongue! Tongue tied (the both of us), she was correct when she said she *didn't* need my help.

The way she sucked and licked my pussy could never be matched. It was like she was massaging my pussy with her fingers and mouth, as her finger was inside me with her tongue, hitting my clit like a drum. *

Jumping up out of my sleep, I looked around to make sure I was in my own bed. I was freaked the fuck *out*! I tried my hardest to fall back asleep in attempt to pick the dream up from where I left off. However, my dreams don't work like that, but I tried.

I was scared to go to her house now, what if it happened? What if I went and *it* didn't happen? I didn't even communicate with her the rest of the weekend. I wrote her in our spiral and told her I had a crazy dream. I think she took it wrong because she was upset. I never got a chance to tell her the whole dream, due to us arguing and never coming back from it!

Nyla started telling me to 'shut up' when I tried to answer questions in class. One day she even asked, *"Why is you even sitting over here by me?"* It was normal for us to get into it, yet this was different, this time the teacher and teacher's aide addressed the situation.

Coach Carr asked, *"What the hell is going on with you two?"*

"That's her!" I blurted out.

"Girl, shut up," Nyla remarked.

"Nah for real, what's going on? Y'all best friends! Why are y'all picking with each other?" Valisha asked.

"We ain't friends no more," Nyla replied.

"Eat them words bitch. I hope you fall and break yo' neck on the basketball court," I said out of anger.

"Earlissa!" Coach Karr and Valisha screamed.

I walked out of class, not giving a fuck about a referral. I wanted to fight that bitch to show her I wasn't 'none of Lani.' I told myself I wouldn't speak to her again and over the next two months, I kept the same energy.

One day, *Valisha* asked her [Nyla] were we talking again, and she shook her head like she wanted to be friends again, but I couldn't forgive her. I couldn't help that people thought we were lowkey talking.

She could never say why she was mad, she would just say, *"Because... she knows why though."*

And I *never* knew a damn thing, but I *knew* I wasn't gone let a bitch play *me*!

Dede

I MET *Deandra* during the summer after sophomore year. *Quanna* got me a job working with her at McDonald's on Southwest Parkway. *Dede* was on vacation when I started, but she came up to the job one day to use the Wi-Fi for a test *(she was a sophomore in college)*.

She asked *Raven* who I was and when did I start etc., trying to get to know me, without my knowing. When she came up there, she had on gray sweats, a Lakers jersey *(Kobe of course)*, a pair of Saucony sneakers, a few necklaces–with a matching bracelet. She had the prettiest smile, dreads *(I call them 'locs, but Africans and Jamaicans say there's a difference)*, and her skin tone was two shades from coal... for some reason I just took to her.

"That's the gay girl I told you about," Quanna whispered in my ear.

"When did you ever tell me about her?" I asked. I had been set on making *Corsair mine*, I didn't recall the conversation.

"Remember, I told you about the girl that call herself 'The Deedster'?" Quanna asked, slightly taking me back.

"Ooooooooooh..."

"Cousin, I told you about the girl that liked me up here."

"You should have said that from jump street, and we'd be talking about something else right now."

"Well bitch, that's her."

Laughingly, I asked, *"Are you sure she came on to you?"*

"You think I'm lying? And what's funny, Lissa?"

"I ain't said nothing, I think yo' ass curious and you wanted her to talk to you, and when she said the slightest thing to you, you got scared because you knew she would take it there with yo' skinny ass."

"I'm in love with Moe, I don't like girls... my sisters do."

I laughed because I know a gay muthafucka when I *see* one. I had been working there for three weeks and *Dede* was back. She was training me on the drive-thru. I was a fast learning and put in for extra shifts, cross training. I was hired to be a cashier, but I wanted to flip burgers *(as they say)*.

I didn't need help or training, I just hated talking through the microphone to the customers. The drive-thru is the same thing as taking orders on the back and front registers, only difference is that I had to greet and 'up-sale' more.

"Can you show me how to modify this #3?" I asked.

"No doubt, shawty," Dede replied.

She came over to help me, walking me through it. I let her finish taking the order while I punched it in.

"Thank you."

"You're good. That's what I'm here for."

I walked over to watch how orders were ran in the drive- thru, letting her lightly trained me on that. The day dragged, but it was almost over and so far, drive-thru was a success. Before the night was over, I had to stock the ice, stock the drive-thru fridge, and mop the register area.

Finally, we slowed down, and I made my list, writing the quantity beside it. I sat it down so I could see how many buckets I would need for the lobby. I went back for my list, but I couldn't find it. In between that incident, two cars pulled into the drive-thru, stopping me from flipping my shit... *over a list*!

I took the orders, immediately going back to looking for my list. Since *Dede* fulfills the orders, I can't hand out the food until she hands it to me. I turned around and *Dede* was coming from the walk-in fridge with *everything* on my list.

"Here [handing me a tray with what I needed and two extras of each items]. Go get your ice, I'll hand these two orders out," she instructed.

I sat the tray down and walked to the back to grab the buckets to fill them with ice. I got the ice and, again, there are more cars in the drive thru, so I sat the buckets down. As soon as the handles left my hands, *Dede* picked them up, filling the ice in the lobby. *She even stocked the drive thru fridge for me!* All I had left to do was fill the ice in the drive-thru and mop... I went to get more ice while she was holding down *'operation drive-thru.'*

By the time I made it back to the front, there were no cars. *Dede* stood in the window texting. She was in my way, but, for whatever reason, I didn't want to say, 'excuse me,' and she take the buckets, leaving me with nothing to do. I bent over to grab and pour the ice in the machine. That's when Dede said,

"You bend from the knees, not your back."

So many thoughts ran through my mind, the main one being: *she was looking at my ass.*

"I know what I'm doing, and I don't care about proper bending, it's time to go and I'm ready to go!" I told her.

"Weeeelllll excuse me, Ms. Hunter."

"How do you know my last name?"

"I know everything that happens around here, I have eyes on, even when I'm gone."

I thanked her for helping me... Well, *really*, for doing all my 'to-go' work. After thanking her, I stood in the drive-thru window, watching her work. She had to mop the front lobby and stock all the sauces. As I was standing in the window watching the cameras in the drive-thru, *Dede* came over to stock her sauces, but *didn't* ask me to move. Instead, we're standing uniform-to-uniform, while she placed several sauces in the right spot. I didn't move, I admired her lips, waiting for her to kiss my pussy.

"I could have moved out your way," I said.

"There was no need, you are good."

My mind started to wonder for a split second, but I didn't want to make myself seem like everywhere I go, there's a female trying to come on to *me*, so I let it go. We talked until my ride pulled up—she noticed before I did. I tried to rush and mop the floor, but again, *Dede* told me *she* would do it for *me*, finishing *my* job.

For the next two months, we flirted and said several things that would have gotten us suspended, *indefinitely*. One day, I went into the walk-in to grab some apple pies out the walk-in. I also used that time to text—so, when the door swung open, I hurried and stashed my phone... *just in case it was a manager*. I did that for nothing, it was *Dede*; she saw me go in the walk-in and wanted to come in, too.

I gathered my [apple] pies, while *Dede felt* on me from behind. I looked at her crazy, causing her to stop. As soon as she took her hands off of me, the walk-in door swung open, and this time, it *was* a manager. She wanted to know *'where the fuck the apple pies were,'* – her exact words. I slid passed them both, *thanking God* we didn't get caught!

I'm not even sure *how* we became a couple–I mean I *know* she asked me to be her girlfriend, I just don't remember when... or *how*. I do remember her texting me, asking me to come over and to grab her some Chinese food from the mall, assuring me that she'd pay me back. I texted before I pulled up so I would know what entry to turn into... in doing *all* the assurance, I still got lost.

Finally, I pulled up to Colony Park. Oh my gosh, it was like going to Alkebulan! Them muthafuckas [Africans] came out like roaches! I called *Dede* because she wasn't coming out fast enough and those *African booty scratchers* started to ask me who was I there for. Once they seen me with *Dede*, they knew there wasn't a chance.

I handed her the food she requested, while telling her that I was just *seconds* from leaving... only because I was swarmed by African roaches. I'm serious–more than 7 muthafuckas came up to me, all knowing each other, not caring because I was someone they'd never seen.

I didn't know she had company so as soon as I walked in, I said, *"You don't gotta pay me back, just eat my pussy when you get done eating."*

"Yooooooo!" Deandrea said laughing.

"What?" I asked.

"My friend is in there fixing my bed," she replied.

A male's voice called from the room. She went to see what he needed, while I made myself comfortable. When she came back, she was laughing. I asked what she was laughing for, and she texted me:

'I went in there thinking he needed help or something and he asked me were you my girlfriend and wanted to know what you look like.'

I couldn't help but laugh out loud because he already knew she had a girlfriend, he just hadn't seen me yet, but he would–I mean he did have to come out the room and walk past me, eventually. He came from the back and saw me sitting at her table and blinked... like he'd seen me in his dreams or something.

"Hello beautiful, nice to me you," he said, waiting on my name.

"I'm Lissa, it's nice to meet you as well." He shook my hand.

"I couldn't get that last bolt off, but I will come back tomorrow and finish. I'll let you two enjoy y'all evening."

They spoke in their native language and said their goodbyes. I went into her room to lay in her bed because I wanted her to *eat in peace.* We talked from the kitchen table to the bedroom. I took my shirt off and unbuttoned my pants, not because I was overly excited to get my pussy ate – it was fucking hot in her place! Just like it is when you're in the club house the Caribbean's throw their parties at. I guess the whole apartment complex was *sharing one box air conditioner.*

Back to the story, *Dede* walked in when I decided to take off my pants. She wasn't expecting to walk in on me – in my bra and panties. She walked in eating her food, she went to sit the food down on the floor. However, she thought about it and said,

"Nah... ima take my food in there because if we step on my food, my fat ass gone be mad."

"You gone eat it anyways!"

"I sure am and ima eat you too!"

I laughed, I got nervous when she said that, even though I knew *that's* what I was there *for*. She came back into the room looking for me to still be standing, but I was laying in the bed with the fan on high.

"It's hot in here, I know. But ima cool you off," Dede said.

"Stop talking and come do it."

She went down to take my panties off. I stopped her and told her to come kiss me before she put her mouth on me because I wasn't going to kiss her afterwards. She laughed and asked me,

"You scared to taste yourself?"

"No... I just think it's nasty."

Face to face, she told me how beautiful I was before she kissed me. She ran her fingers through my long hair and continued to kiss me. I lightly kicked the bed, trying to fight the aching pains between my legs.

She kissed me *all* over – *twice* in the places she couldn't wait to suck and lick. Slowly, she slid her hands under my ass and pulled me to the edge of the bed, pulling my panties down in the process. She lifted up each leg, starting with the right one. My leg came out of my panties, causing my panties to fall down to my left thigh. She didn't put my legs down, she stared in between my legs instead.

My *wetness* started to run down to my ass and onto the bed. I lifted my head and my leg to grab my panties off me, because they were wet as well. She kissed me and noticed my titties jiggling from me shaking. She grabbed my titties, so I grabbed her dreads as I was removing my left titty from my bra and placed her mouth on my nipple. My heart sped up, my pussy was throbbing extra hard, it was like I heard my pussy through my ears, and I shook even *harder*.

Wrapping my legs around her ass, I pulled my bra off so she could suck my right titty, then run her tongue across both. I took her left hand and placed it on my pussy, giving her access to my playground. She rubbed her thumb up and down on my clit then looked at me and said,

"You wet as fuck, yoooooo!"

"I'll wipe it off…I don't want yo' face to be all messy," I replied, in shame.

"Who said I didn't want a beautiful mess on my face?"

I didn't answer that, I focused on my breathing so that I wouldn't have a panic attack I just *knew* she would deliver. *Dede*, now on her knees, placed her hands on my stomach with weight and went in *full throttle*. I couldn't move. She had the tongue of a *lemur*, the main one for eating and a second tongue hidden under the first! I heard her slurping and smacking *over* my moans. I don't remember how many times I came in her mouth – she just *wouldn't* stop. I was the wishing well that would quench her everlasting thirst.

"Stop…!" I moaned out.

"Nope I'm tryna eat yo' pussy better than Vince did."

'Where did that even come from?' I asked myself. I pushed her face *deeper* into my pussy for the childish shit she had just said.

"Sooooo you wanna push my face into it? Alright… How about this?" She placed two fingers deep inside of me.

For seconds, I was trying to catch my breath. It was uncomfortable, but I tried to fuck both fingers anyways. She realized it was slightly uncomfortable and took one [finger] out and then put her face back in my *pudding*. I felt her hitting something inside my pussy and I quickly moved up in the bed, causing her to climb up on the bed… but she *hooked* inside of me, so there was no escaping. I begged and pled with her; I didn't know much about a *g-spot*. I knew where it was located, but I didn't know if I was going to *pee*, *cum*, or *orgasm*. From the porn I saw, the women did a little of all *three*! I didn't want to experience a tsunami just yet, a muthafucka gotta *earn* that–plus I'd be embarrassed.

The uncontrollable shaking started again, moving the whole bed... I begged her again to stop. It felt so good! I was scared to release what I was feeling, so tears flowed with the orgasm. I screamed and cried, riding her face until I could bring myself to *unleash* her. I was squeezing her head with my thighs, wrapping her hair around in my hand, *and didn't even notice it.*

"You wanna let me go now?" Dede asked.

"I can't stop shaking," I replied, still not releasing her hair. When I finally let her up, she came and laid on the side of me, trying to hold me. Instead, I pushed her over and climbed on top of her.

I said I wouldn't kiss her after she tasted me but that was *then*! I had a sudden *urge* to kiss her. In doing so, I discovered I *tasted* like a little bit of *heaven*. I kissed her again like she kissed my pussy while grinding on her. She didn't want to be touched, though–she had more *'off limits'* spots than Christian Grey–which was fine with me, because I *still* received the *ultimate satisfaction*. She was horny as fuck, but since she got her satisfaction from pleasing her lovers, she went back down to eat some more.

This time, I was a *tad* bit more prepared. I put my finger inside my pussy and let her taste it... while I joined her.

"I thought it was 'nasty'?" Dede asked as she licked her lips.

I wanted to answer her, but I *showed* her instead. While she was licking her lips, I flicked my tongue, like, *'come here.'* She came in for a kiss, but I licked her tongue to show her, there wasn't *nothing* nasty about me.

I laid on my stomach and told her to give me a massage, she went straight for my ass. Her ass is *bigger* than mine, so I'm not sure why she was *so* turned on, but she was. She caressed my ass and finally began to rub my back and my shoulders. She took her right hand and slid it down my back, grabbed my ass, before putting a finger inside of me. I arched up just enough for her hand to move up and down. I rocked back and forth while her finger was going in and out of me... grinding slowly. I had her hand wet, so she decided her face and hand should switch places.

"I'm not gone eat yo ass, but I'll kiss it," she said out of nowhere.

"What the fuck!?"

"Hey, I'm just saying."

I flopped face down on the bed, pretending as if I didn't want her to eat my pussy. That's when she opened my legs, planting soft kisses on my ass, working her way to the center of me. I flipped over because I didn't want my ass all in her face, she ate my pussy until the cream and cum was all gone – I *love* the way she sucked and licked mu pussy at the same time! I won't lie, she put me to sleep; I woke up and it was 8:16 PM, or some shit.

We were already a couple, but sex was the start of our very toxic, on-and-off relationship. Shit was so deep; I couldn't hide me being in love with a girl. People noticed at work, my people noticed at home, the students at school, and I *hated* that shit *(the fact that I was in love with a girl)*!

I started to not take our relationship serious, since I was still in high school, and she was in college. Quickly, I began to not trust her, but it was *really* because I didn't trust myself. I don't remember the heartache, but she does, and she described a love... I remember being shunned and the sex... *we both also remember the first time differently.*

The Way She Remembered Us

I remember the first day that I saw *Lissa* like it was yesterday. She was wearing the same exact thing that I was wearing, but she made that McDonalds uniform look so good. The lust I felt was instant and palpable. She was gorgeous, even beneath the scowl she was wearing.

There was something about the seriousness of her expression that was inviting to me. I guess I have always loved a challenge. I don't remember how I got her number or even when I got her number. I *do* remember long phone calls and text message chains.

I remember meeting her, up at Burger King during the time she was going to Driving School. *Lissa* had me acting the fool and pretending to be grown. I was older than her, but she had me open and feeling out of my depth. I recall the first time that we fucked. I thought of cleaning it up and saying I remember the first time I made love to her, but nah–I remember the first time that we *fucked*.

She got dropped off at my apartment by her grandmother, I think. It was a late summer afternoon. I don't remember even trying to be the *polite* African American West Indian that I was raised to be. I didn't offer her a drink or something to eat... I was after that pussy! I was wearing a black du-rag, a white wife beater, basketball shorts, and she was wearing nothing.

We didn't even make it to the bed. We fucked on the floor – I remember because she got rug burns. In retrospect, I'm not even sure if I knew how to fuck *then*, but I gave her what I had at that time. In return, her pussy *cried me a rive*r. This was long ago, and I'm still not sure when I fell in love with *Lissa*. It could have been at that very moment, or it could have been the time I rode my Honda Bicycle Percival, aka '*Percy*,' onto the highway over to West Lynwood.

That night, we fucked in an alley on a bed of grass. *That night* I realized that I was allergic to grass. The pussy was worth it, though! The adrenaline of the moment. I could have been bit by a dog, caught by a resident, arrested maybe, or a crackhead could have stepped on my foot!

I left the situation with some good ass sex and a little skin irritation from the grass. *Lissa* and I attempted a relationship at a time when people weren't yet ready to admit that same sex relationships could flourish. And at our ages, the sex, while *extraordinary* for what it was, just wasn't enough to keep us together.

We fizzled out sometime after that, and now, all that are left are the memories. I smile whenever I remember the *wild* shit, she had me doing. I fell far down the rabbit hole where she was concerned. Thank you for the memories, Ms. Hunter. *I think I just might love you forever.*

-From the Deedster.

MiMi

'Mimi' is mentioned often, she was after *Vince, Corsair,* and *Dede,* but I met her while dating *Vince.* When I found out she was gay, she thought I wouldn't want to be cool anymore –honestly, that made me open up to her more.

Females slapping each other's ass back then was the thing, so I had touched that big round muthafucka *plenty* of times. I was still with *Vince* when I told her I liked her, although I didn't fuck with her until after *Vince* and I broke up. After she ate my pussy in her car, she wanted to be my girlfriend, I was cool with that.

I liked her a lot... I didn't know how to treat her; I really didn't know *how* to be in a relationship with a woman. I was so drawn to her. I would threaten to beat her up when I thought she was lying. Thinking on it, I guess I wanted to be the *nigga,* not knowing there was only one role to play. She got tired of my shit and stopped fucking with me.

Some time went by *(like a year)* ... I don't know how I found out, but I heard she had a baby. I wasn't hurt, but I wanted to *hear it from the horses' mouth.* She confirmed it to be true. I said 'congratulations,' and was going to leave it alone, but she wanted to catch up. *Mimi* went on to tell me about what we used to have, and how she missed me.

I missed her too, but I didn't wanna deal with baby-daddy drama. I had no kids, so I didn't have any baby-daddy drama to match that energy and decided to just be friends. She texted me this long ass text message a day after we started back talking:

I miss you a lot. I really want you and that pussy all to myself. You have a beautiful body... I think I'm the only person that knows how beautiful you are when you smile. I have love for you, Lissa, I'm not playing games with you. I miss tasting you, putting my tongue all in that little fat pussy. I want that pussy in my face, Lissa. Ride my face until you cum, then let me suck that cum out of you. I deserve that pussy. Send me a picture of that pussy, I want you creaming. Let me eat that pussy from the back, baby. I want that wet pussy all over me...

My pussy was wet as *fuck–I knew what her mouth would do*. Her words held much weight! I sent her a picture, like she asked. I wasn't going to fuck her, though. Her 'sexting' me was cool for the time being, but I told myself I was going to take a break from sex. Several failed relationships – sex was not the trick; it just made the relationship tolerable.

- I started writing this last night and had to stop... I felt the sudden *urge* to be fucked, but no one was around. I found myself sitting down at my computer, grabbing the nearest phone to me (*I have three*) and my headphones, and then I headed to the bed. I fought with myself on whether I should or not – eventually I said, 'fuck it.'

Doubling back to get some latex gloves, I hurried and jumped back into the bed. I am not a fan of porn, but within writing this and talking to my sex slave, I wanted to feel some pain–and flow like the river. I wanted to grab my black butt plug [that *hasn't* been in my ass] to stick in-and-out of my pussy... that's the closest thing I have to a toy (I hate toys, they just don't feel *real* enough).

I told myself I needed to *feel myself, for myself*. I went to google and typed in: 'ebony lesbians with pretty pussies.' I clicked the first search result that popped up–as long as it wasn't Pornhub, I was cool with it. As soon as the website loaded, my eyes went to roaming. Hell, I didn't know if I wanted to watch the videos on page one or the ads above them. I went 5 videos down, telling myself I was coming back to the first one.

Eventually, I finally went back to page one, video one, after 12 videos. I would tell y'all the 12 videos I watched, but from the titles a muthafucka will judge me *hard* lol. By the third video, I put my glove on, ready to feel my insides.

OMG!! *I was wet as fuck!* Don't get me wrong, I've always known it was a waterpark down there, but *got damn! Mimi* always said it was a 'honeypot,' but I truly didn't know for myself. I've never been digging for honey for real, I never go *that* deep. Through the glove, I was *losing* it–the sensation felt like *raw sex...* I've never bought that, *"I can't feel you through a rubber"* bullshit.

I began talking to myself, asking myself *crazy* ass questions like, *"If I looked at my glove, would it be blood or Milk Marie...? Is this why they be going crazy...?"*

"I know this why muthafuckas go crazy!"

...I laughed because for a second, I felt like I was caught, or being watched – must have been the ancestors, because I was home alone. I laid sideways, placing my middle finger inside. I did not like that I was about to violate myself, but my pussy felt *so* good... *like bro, I can't make this shit up!* I slowly went in-and-out, rubbing my clit on every other 'in' motion, applying pressure to the hood of my pussy. Then I heard *Chevy's* voice saying, *"Yeaaaah! Grip that dick!"*

...When I gripped my finger, I asked myself if I could still squirt without being penetrated. Thinking about my top five while watching porn got me 'there,' but I stopped... I didn't want to finish, *I just needed to know if I still had it.*

I was deeper in my thoughts than the porn, but there was a piece that caught my eyes: the girl was eating her best friend's pussy–her eyes told it all. They talked to each other... there was so much passion in that clip, it took me back to one out of the *many* times *Cortez* went *crazy* on my pussy.

Cortez

SHIT WITH THIS BITCH was inevitable, too. *'We started off as close friends, somehow, she turned into my girlfriend...'* I can't say I was 'in love,' but I did love her, due to our friendship, and it just carried over. She was insecure of the fact that I was bi, she's a dyke/stud–*whatever you want to call it* – I call her 'boy' (not *a* boy, just 'boy').

Quick rundown on *Cortez* if you've never read my work:

Cortez started out dating my ex-friend. The ex-friend thought I liked *Cortez*, on the account of when they got into it at school, she was wrong, and told her. She then took it upon herself to say some shit like, *"Well, y'all must like each other"* and *"Y'all must be fucking..."* that stupid shit caused us to fall the fuck out. Still, *Cortez* and I didn't fuck around until *years* later.

Also, she has a brother–he liked me my freshman year... I guess you can say I led him on because I *really* didn't like him, he just kept me entertained and I let him kiss me one day after walking me home. Well, I know I lead him on because I told him, *"I love you too."* I didn't *not* want to say it back. At the time, I just didn't want to be rude.

Anyways, I can't think of a time when *Cortez* wasn't eating on *my* pussy! One of my favorite times would have to be a few weeks into our making 'it' [us] official. She was high and two shots in. I drank wine back then, and liquor on a night I was going out, so I didn't join in–plus I was a solo smoker. I laid on my stomach while she laid across my back, smoking. We were talking about work *(we both worked at Walmart, but not the same location)* but I really wanted her to hurry up, because I knew that head was going to be *amazing*.

Rolling off of me to put the blunt out, she began to tug on my pants, letting me know to take them muthafuckas *off*. I usually come in and drop my clothes, but after being walked in on, I stopped doing that. I stood up to unbutton my pants and pull them down. *Cortez* slid her right hand through my pussy like a credit card.

"Why you already soaking?" Cortez asked.

"I'm not," I replied, laughing.

As I bent down to step out of them [pants], *Cortez* came to the edge of the bed – but I didn't think anything of it. As soon as I came back up, she went down... I hate getting head while standing up, it makes my knees give out – but she was under me *just right*! Her tongue was up *in* my pussy like a *dick*. In-and-out she went, I done Kegels on her tongue. I leaned her head back so that I could place my knees on the bed and fuck her face. I felt myself about to cum. That's when I got off her face, laid back, and let her come put her face *into* me. She threw the comforter over her head as she went down to taste me. I felt her *lips* on my *lips* and pressed up against hers, *harder*. I wanted her to *suck* my pussy, *eat* my pussy, then *lick* my pussy... she *did*, but not in *that* order.

Cortez continued tongue-fucking me, then she slowly transitioned to licking my pussy. It was the basic up-and-down motion, but it was still *amazing*! Switching it up, she began to moan while she ate my pussy – straight *carpet muncher*! It was when she began to suck my pussy that made me *lose* it. As she was sucking my clit, she looked me in my eyes and asked, *"You like that shit, huh?"*

"Yesssssss daddy! Suck this pussy," I moaned out. She sucked my clit harder while licking my vagina opening. *"I'm 'bout to cum!"*

"Keep fucking my face. You bet not stop!"

"I'm cum... fuuuuuuck–I'm cummin'!" Screaming like them white hoes that be faking it.

"Yeah bitch," Cortez remarked, like she *knew* she defeated me.

I was finished for the moment. That was an orgasm waiting to happen. I stopped her–until it passed, then I let her continue sucking the cum *out* of my pussy. As she sucked on my pussy, I made her tell me she was 'my bitch,' while I grinded my hips in a *left-right-up-down* motion. I felt myself getting ready to explode *again,* but I couldn't take her mouth anymore. I pushed her head up – hell, she needed to breathe anyways.

"Why you do that?" Cortez asked.

"Put your fingers in me!"

As she inserted her ring and middle finger, I *squirted.*

"Really in my eyes?" She asked.

"I didn't know that was going to happen," I replied, embarrassed as fuck.

We laughed. I watched her doze off and I decided to take a little nap myself. I wasn't drinking or smoking, so I slept light. I woke up forty-five minutes later, slipped up from under her and left. She called me when she woke up – but that was damn near midnight, and I was asleep then.

Shit started to get rocky after 8 months, and I was pulling away at this point. She wanted to be *so* 'hard,' but she was a crybaby, also the 'fuck up.' *We all know how I feel about a bitch tryna play me! Ain't gone do it!*

I don't do 'phone checks,' meaning, I mind my own business. I checked her phone before, on the account of her best friend being *too* friendly. Muthafuckas tell on themselves... if I am love and light, how long do you think something is going to remain hidden? I swear, I heard a voice or something that said, *check Facebook.* Not the phone... but *Facebook*! That shit fucked me up. I kept telling myself, *no, don't do it,* but my heart began beating fast and a muthafucka started to *feel* funny.

The first time I checked her phone, it wasn't bad as I'm making it out to be—the bitch was just *extra* friendly! I checked her Facebook, and this ugly muthafucka (*Cortez*) was doing the *fucking* most! It was bitches *all through* that muthafucka. I didn't trip, I just ended shit – I wasn't feeling her like that since the 'best friend' shit, so that was all the ammo I needed.

She called and begged so much. I let her pick me up a month after the 'best friend' shit–*just* so she could eat my pussy. She thought 'us chilling' that last time put an 'okay' stamp on everything... and it didn't - I just wanted some head. *Cortez* told me how much she missed me while she sucked out my soul, but I was already on to the next bitch.

Roaming Around

I CHILLED AFTER *Cortez*; it was about three years later when I fucked with another female. I wasn't even *trying* to fuck with her, but *Ebony* made it hard not to. That bitch was *crazy*, so I left that bitch alone... I let her give me head while *Mexico* and I split for a few months, and she started acting like she was my woman... shit was *crazy*.

Cortez moved to The Summit's [apartment], where my sister lived. I brought some weed from her cousin that was over there so that we could match. She had a girl, so it was *seriously* a smoke session... but after that, she asked [in a text] me if she could eat my pussy.

I ignored her message for three days before I texted back *'no.'*

People hated me for being with her, they thought I should be with a *'girly*-girl' since I was 'mannish' enough on my own.

Mexico and I patched shit up, we moved in together again–then *he* ended up moving out. I stayed in that place for a year, and then I found a house in the Avenues. I stopped fucking with him [Mexico]–he got a new girlfriend–I started fucking with *Marqus* again. We were forever connected, but toxic... *Mexico* and I... I was tired of it but didn't know how to break the cycle... we *couldn't* break the cycle.

I started working at the hospital, and my sister told *Mexico* that it was my third day there. The first day out of training, he popped up. I had already met *three* bitches by then, I was just debating on which one I was going to let eat my pussy–although I wouldn't mind an *all-female* orgy.

I left them three alone once *Mexico* got back into the picture. However, *Ebony* didn't give up – she didn't give a fuck! *There* was *one* black girl at the hospital that tried to talk to me, but there was *something* about her I just couldn't fuck with–I did rub *all* over that big ass though. *(Small world; her and Mexico started fucking around four years later, I'm still cool with her, though... I don't care about shit like that too much)*

We moved back in together [*Mexico* and I], but I felt like I could have a girlfriend on the side – I swear, I don't consider it *cheating*... that's when I first met *Bella* and *Ryan*.

Ryan is a soothsayer, all *spiritual* and shit. I told her I didn't want to fuck with her head, but she wanted to *try it* anyways. *Mexico* and I decided to separate [for real] and I went back to talking to my many women. *Women eat pussy better than men, anyways.*

I needed to feel a woman's mouth on my pussy... *ASAP*!

I continued to meet women, on top of *Mimi* and I catching back up. I won't lie, I even though about letting *Ebony* eat my pussy, but she can't control her emotions – that bothers me. Besides, it was *way* too many bitches to choose from, I didn't have to *settle* or just pick *one*. I am who I am!

Head From The Head Doctor

THE PROBLEM WITH PEOPLE, they will say *anything* just to spark a conversation. Meaning, they *talk* just to *talk*; there's no way in hell the doctors should have known I was *gay*. But, I guess, when you talk to more than one person at the hospital, the word *will* travel like God-speed.

I told her that I wouldn't ever *speak* on it–but I *never* said I wouldn't *write* about it, and since I'm writing about it–she'll remain *nameless*, like a few others... for *professional* purposes.

This bitch was *soooooo* mean to me when I started working at the hospital. You know how it is when you start a job for the first time – you try to be as *nice* as possible – when you are *really* raised off *Boosie*–and will *'set that muthafucka off!'*

She's a nurse with her BSN. I felt like she thought because she had a *degree*, and I was a *cashier*, that she could talk to me *any* kind of way. I let her make it a whole month before I began to *refuse* her in my [checkout] line. She had the nerve to ask me *why I don't like to ring her up.* I ignored her. She would always rush me, she came in the cafe talking loudly, she talked on the phone while being rung up, and expected me to *constantly* repeat shit to her.

She came in one day and asked, *"Did I do something to wrong you?"*

"Brina, she's talking to you," I said to the other cashier, ignoring her. She looked at me like she wanted to mow me down, she was so pissed she walked away.

"You are so mean... but you're not mean to me, so it's funny," Brina said, with her squeaky ass voice.

"No! I've been really nice to her, that bitch tries to treat me like a slave. She stays talking crazy to me, she got these white girls thinking they can raise their voices. And she knows got damn well she's supposed to open her box to show me her food and every time I ask her, she says 'it's germs in the air.' She really just wanna eat my pussy."

"That's true, that bitch weird."

I'm unsure of *which* part Brina agreed with me on, but I'm thinking *everything...* she's been there longer than me–*plus she was into women herself.*

The nurse hadn't even ordered before she came over there fucking with me. I looked around and she was just now putting in an order. After she ordered and got her food, she came into my line, and I totaled her out. She wanted to say something, but I walked away to talk to Mr. Eddie. Mr. Eddie knows I like women (somewhat), and he was always sure to tell me who was *gay* up there. That damn maintenance man knew *everything...* But that was all I needed to know, I told myself, *'Ima talk real stupid to this ho!'* It was time for Brina to leave, and with her [Brina] counting down her drawer, I had no choice but to let this bitch come into my line.

"Again, did I do something to you?" The nurse asked.

"You rude as fuck! I'm tired of being nice to y'all. If you can't work under pressure without being a bitch, you should have gone to school for something else," I said, ready to fight!

"Are you serious right now?!"

"Your total is $6.77, ma'am."

I wanted to be cordial, but the bitch wanted to play stupid... so, she could fuck off. I was talking to Brina as she was counting down her drawer, and noticed the nurse sitting at the closest table to the register. I turned my back to her so I couldn't see her staring at me, *being weird and shit*. She didn't take her eyes off me; I could feel them *bugged* eyes *piercing* through my *back*. Brina grabbed her deposit bags, energy drink, and her cart before telling me she'd see me tomorrow.

She [nurse] was doing *everything* to get me to look her way, *but that's how the devil works*. I stayed in one section until she left, collecting my thoughts, and questioning myself – for the fact that I wanted her to eat my pussy for giving me such a hard time. Looking for the rest of the day, it was time to start pulling and stocking products while time continued to pass by. I pulled the doors three minutes early thinking no one would come in that short period of time... however, I was wrong.

Beating on the door is the nurse that makes my ass itch, yet she's also the *same* person I want to *taste* me. Ignoring her like I do best, I kept grabbing products for next day's shift... the knocks got harder. I opened the door considering she had merely a little over a minute of time remaining before I officially closed. Letting her catch the door, she smacked her lips.

"Maaaan! Don't come in here smacking ya fucking lips, I didn't have to open the door!" I shouted.

"No need to shout yet, I just wanted some fresh spinach before you closed."

I told her to 'grab it and go,' keeping it short, but she didn't listen. I turned around and we walked right into each other. At the moment I wanted to push her down, *in that same moment, I her to kiss my pussy.* We could do neither, due to the cameras–I rushed her off instead.

"We're closed now. The spinach is free, just leave," I told her.

"I want to pay for it."

"Please go, you making my head hurt."

"Well, when are you going to be heading outside?"

"You asked that like you want to fight."

She began to walk away from me. Once she made it to the door, she said,

"I'll be at your car waiting when you get off little girl."

My first thought was to chase her down to kick her ass, but I figured: if she *were* waiting on me after work like she said, I could keep my job and kick her ass *off* the clock. I was power cleaning, deep thinking, and ready to hit the doors. I ran *Brad* down with my cart, stomped on *Darnell's* foot trying to get into the elevator. I was in such a rush; I dropped my deposit without the information needed. I could have opened the safe, however, I had a meeting in the parking lot.

I text my boss to let her know about the deposit, my heart was pounding as I scoped the hospital floors. She [nurse] had me watching my back. I made it to the parking lot, this bitch was *really* waiting on me like she said she would.

I told myself: *I'm bout to kill this ho.* I started speed walking [*cause what's up?*]. She was talking but I did not hear her, due to me being across the street. As I get closer, I hear her saying, *"Don't swing on me, I just wanna talk."*

I responded with a shout because we're still many feet apart: *"I don't know you... for you to be waiting on me, and you rude... you better get to saying what the fuck you want before I get in 'touching distance.'"*

Within so many feet, something told me not to hit her, rather hear her out. It was as if she knew I had changed my mind, because the gibberish in the distance became complete silence within the parking lot. The closer I got, the more comfortable I became with her body language; however, it wasn't enough for me to let up–all the way.

"What you want, woman?" I asked.

She didn't answer me, she let her eyes talk until she was comfortable enough to say what she felt. I avoid staring into people's eyes, yet my mind wouldn't stop telling me to read her.

"You can taste my pussy, if you want," I told her in *the softest* voice.

"I'll kiss it for now... I want to pay for it."

She got on her knees as if she were about to give me *full lip service, nose all in my pussy*, and planted a kiss in the middle of my pants. As she got up, she began to tell me about a proposition she had:

She told me that if she could eat my pussy in front of her husband, she would pay me *two days her pay*.

I've never been the type to take money for services, it's usually deeper than that. I told her I would think about it. She put something in my pocket and grabbed my pussy before walking away. I watched her black scrubs disappear into the night as I stood in shock, *replaying the moment we just shared.*

The drive home was rather long, with nothing but nature for sound. I *wanted* her to eat my pussy, yet I *didn't* want her money. Then again, *who* am I to turn it *down*? The next couple of days at work was awkward – she began to pop up more, Mr. Eddie even asked me was she my girlfriend, since she was sweet on *me* now.

"Have you thought about what I said?" She asked.

"I have and give me until the weekend to think about it, please."

"I'll call you Friday and if you're up for it, I'll have my husband pick you up around 9 PM."

"Yes ma'am, I'll let you know my answer by Friday morning."

I didn't want to be seen talking to her since everyone knew I hated her, including my boss. Friday came, *'it wasn't about the money,'* is all I kept telling myself. The phone rang and I declined it, I shot a text to let her know I'd be ready. I declined the call for the fact: if I would have talked to her on the phone, I would have talked myself out of it, playing shy like I didn't want them (her *and* her husband) between my legs. I texted her the address around 7:45 PM, however, I started getting ready at 6... it never fails, when I'm in a rush, I tend to move slow.

Her husband pulled up 15 minutes early in a black 2018 Challenger–fully loaded. I admired his sweet ride, he had it a *year* early. I hadn't put on my dress yet, so I ran to the door in my black silk robe to let him know I'd be out in 7 minutes, tops.

He asked, *"Am I here to pick you up?"*

"Again sir, give me about 7 minutes and I'll be back out."

"Damn, we gone have some fun with you, don't worry I'll be a gentleman until we return to headquarters," he said as he rolled up the window, being a *smart ass*, matching my energy.

I came back out in 10 minutes. As soon as I stepped on the porch to lock the door, he got out the car, waiting on me to get closer before he opened the door. He complimented me on my small red dress and clear platforms. I complimented him on his deep blue, pin-striped suit. I got in and he *gazed* at me before closing the door. I was nervous as fuck, so I made small conversation.

"I'm Lissa, and you are?"

"You may call me 'Sir' for now, you will hear my queen scream my name..."

I said nothing else until we pulled up to Pelican's. As before, he opened my door, but this time, he waited for me to lock arms so *he* could lead the way. As we entered, the hostess noticed him, quickly guiding us to his wife. I didn't know she was *beautiful like that*... I stared in awe, then I snapped back to reality because I didn't know who to sit next to.

"Hello beautiful, how was your ride?" She asked.

"It was quiet."

Her greeting me, made me feel like I should sit next to her. I walked past the table to get to the left of her–that's when I noticed the split in her dress and *immediately* noticed that the split ran up to her thighs. I wanted to reach out and touch her – instead, I just looked, holding in my thoughts.

As we sat down, she told me how beautiful I looked *outside* of my work clothes, while rubbing the areas of my body that *weren't* covered by fabric. Pelican's was just a place to meet and converse before the night got *started*.

Enjoying the conversations at hand, we ordered food, just because we sat there longer than expected. *Sir* ordered the cold-water lobster with scallops, steak and sauteed asparagus in white wine. The lovely lady (once the 'rude bitch') ordered calamari with oysters on a half shell. I wasn't hungry, so I ordered a teriyaki beef kabob. White wine and water quenched the thirst of us all. Time never slowed down, but I refused to fall asleep in bed with them, so I suggested we get a *move* on.

I rode with the wife this time. Like her husband, she opened *and* closed the door for me. I sat in the front, needing to see her beauty *and* body.

Her husband told her that he would go to the ATM, and then he'd be home. He then proceeded with a *request* of her: to make sure she doesn't *taste* the *dessert* before he can watch. I laughed, but I knew she wasn't going to listen; she'd been waiting *too long*.

She agreed to drive straight to the house–she failed to mention she was taking the *long* way. As soon as she got into her black-on-black 2018 Altima, she gave me the look the *lion gives a zebra before the chase begins*. I sat with my legs closed tight, but I wanted to open my legs and let her eat before the feast. She put on 105.7 FM, letting the music clear the air, gently pulled out the parking lot. We went down Midwestern Parkway to go by Christy's Toy Box.

Once we parked, I took off my seat belt thinking we were going inside. She leaned over, turning me sideways while pulling me close to her. She kissed my thighs, rubbing my left thigh with one hand, choking me with the other. Turned on, I sat on the arm rest, pulling my dress up some more before sitting down. I opened my legs, pulling her by her neck to eat up this mess she just made.

"Fuuuuuuck!" is all I could scream while falling back.

"Fuuuuuuck! You taste so good," she said, mocking me.

"Put yo' tongue in my pussy." She teased me with her tongue, quick in and-outs causing me to fuck her face... I needed more. *"Please stop!"* I begged.

"I'll stop for now, I'm not far from home."

She didn't stay far; we passed her house twice getting to Christy's Toy Box. They had a beautiful home, in-ground pool, and one of the rooms looks out to the street–there's no brick around it like the rest of the house, just glass! Every item in the house complimented another piece, the Feng-Shui flowed, that turned me on even more. I sat in the living room waiting on her to come back from the guest house. Upon her return, she came back with three bags. She handed me two of the bags that I couldn't open until they took me home. She poured up some wine, her husband 'pulled up in time' (her words not mine).

The door opened and the wife began to bark out orders.

"Drink the wine and get on your knees before our guest," she demanded as she handed him a glass. The way she was talking, you would have thought she was serving him out of a pet's bowl. I continued to sip, thinking *maybe I should drink mine fast as well*, she made me nervous all over again.

He drank the wine and crawled before me, waiting for his next order. I closed my legs so hard, my knees banged up against each other–louder than the bell of liberty. She came up behind him to hold and open my legs.

"You know what to do, John," she instructed.

"Ma'am, may I?" He asked me. But he didn't wait on me to answer, he was face deep in my pussy mumbling, *"may I fuck yo world up?!"*

As his wife stood behind him, placing pressure onto me, she licked her lips, flicked her tongue, and moaned. She snapped her fingers, like a dog he shook his head, coming to a complete stop. She told him to hold my legs. I thought he was going to hold my legs down. Walking behind the couch, he pulled them up as if he were going to *flip* me. Nobody undressed, yet my dress was damn near above my head... with my feet. Her tongue was *harder* than a dick when she slid it in!

The tip of her tongue went straight in, then she curled it and rammed it inside. I was closer to 'orgasm heaven,' so she let up. As soon as 'the shakes' stopped, she put her tongue back in as deep as she could, sliding it down to the bottom wall of my pussy, kissing my ass cheeks. I pushed her head even deeper inside my pussy—at the same time, I fucked her face. As the juices began to run, her tongue ran behind it.

She lowered herself from sitting dog position to Indian-style. I thought she was finished, but she was *full* of *surprises*. She kept sucking my pussy, however, you could hear her hands in a bag. I could hear a lot of *rumbling* – a condom opened, then it sounded like somebody was cutting hair. John started to cuss and moan – I was scared to look up. At this point, I *knew* it was a vibrator, I just had never *felt* one.

"Take her clothes off, I wanna see you suck her titties," she demanded John. *'Yes Ma'am'* was all he said before ripping my clothes off. He began to lick my ears and neck, massaging my titties before sucking each nipple. *Two mouths... licking and sucking!* I had no choice at this point but to cum *all* over *both* mouths. I grabbed the pillows as her tongue quickly went in and out my pussy. I couldn't hold it anymore, I let the water flow until there was no more. They both loved that shit. She got up to share what was left of the juices with him, sticking her fingers inside of me.

Her titties ended up in my mouth, somehow. She sat down on my lap, wrapping her legs around me. Her body was perfect; like dark chocolate that *melted* in any area of light... big perky titties, with *thhhheeeeee fattest ass*!

She sat there holding me as if we were in love, but honestly, I think she missed being *with* a woman. To prove my theory, I wanted to see if she had that same energy with her husband. Speaking of her husband, he was so into what we had going on, he was fucking the couch, 'pulsating' some would call it.

"Go to the guest bedroom and wait for us," she told John.

Ryan

RYAN is the prettiest woman I've ever been connected with.... Inside and out, fully *divine*, and *blessed* by the *Gods*. Spiritual as fuck, at peace with self–and all things surrounding her.

Ryan is as light as the sun, has the dreadlocks like *Medusa*, face tattoos–with the *prettiest* skin to match. Full lips with hazel green eyes, with a *mind* out of this *world*.

I could sit up here and say it was a 'physical thing,' but *it most definitely was not*. I'm nowhere in *her* league – that's the truth. My mind just so happens to be as beautiful as she is. We all know *energy* is everything. Yet, when two beautiful souls and minds link up, its *pleasure* and *pain*, two of my most *favorite* things.

Ryan just dropped out of the sky like most angels do, knowing my soul needed healing and reassurance. I wanted the peace she had... she was patient. She didn't care about *Bella*, *Brandy*, *Mimi*, or any other bitch. She always told me if we were meant to the cross lines (I felt we shouldn't), it would happen anyway due to the creator's plans–plus she manifested us growing in *love* and peace (mainly peace).

I've always been a force to be reckoned with, but she taught me about *me*, and I know that's crazy... she let me know it was okay to be the sexual being I was. Energy was *felt*, I've never been flipped inside-out like this. She taught me *Feng Shui*, the transfer of energy, and how to block negative energy before it reaches touching distance.

Her body? Trust me, I'll get there. When I say I was afraid to undress around her (y'all know Ima *naked* muthafucka), it wasn't easy for me.

Ryan was the female that pushed me to make it work with the other bitches that I was choosing. She always wanted me to get *more* from the women, *not just my pussy ate*. So, when I was nice to you bitches, thank *Ryan* because I've never thought about giving a bitch more than my pussy–and that's the truth!

She came over one day while my kids were at school. As soon as she pulled up, I threw on a big shirt so I wouldn't be my normal naked self. Walking into the yard, I heard *Ryan* say how my house needed to be cleansed. She couldn't have been more *right*. Mexico and I brought demons that refused to leave, on top of the apartments being erected on top of an old cemetery–once being a slave house that Joe and Frank owned. (Kemp and Kellwest)

"I think I deserve to taste you Renee," Ryan said as she walked in and began to undress.

"Damn, you don't even know if I was gone decline. You didn't greet me or nothing, freaky ass."

"Now is not the time to be scared Earlissa. You talk all that shit–I wanna see what you made of and what you taste like."

Ryan tied her hair up into a wick that resembled a palm tree. That shit was funny, but there *was* a beach side-view as she stood in the nude. Her yellow skin was glowing, her titties set *exactly* right, an inch of fat on her stomach, thick thighs, fair hips, with an ass out of this *world*! She had light stretch marks on her ass, she was perfect...

I wasn't scared of *Ryan*, I just never wanted to cross those *thin* ass lines. I just needed one person that didn't wanna fuck me behind everything that was in front of us. I have dog-ass ways... for that reason alone, I wanted her to save her energy.

As she begged me to be as open as I should, her titties jumped, shook, and vibrated with each word. I threw her the nearest thing to me (a blanket), wanting her to cover up. I just didn't want to fuck with my *spiritual coach* on that level. I'm not always the best person to be around. My energy can get so low, I will turn negative in *the* worst ways. Not wanting to rub that onto her, she felt rejected... however, she didn't give up. The energy she gave off reminded me of *Ebony*.

"Energy doesn't lie. I know you want me... I'ma touch you in all the places that's crying out for me. At any time if you feel uncomfortable, I'll stop," Ryan informed.

I walked in after her and sat on the edge of the bed – she stood between my legs. She reached for my phone to turn on the music. When she reached over, she smelled of *jasmine* and *lavender*. I tried to ignore the fact that she put her titties in my face. At the same time, I told myself: *give her what she wants... ...give that bitch what she wants!*

I grabbed her lower back to bring her closer to me–as if she weren't close enough already. I wanted to feel her ass, since she was in a *touching* mood. I thought about eating her pussy – *and I don't even fuck around like that*. I put my finger in the crack of her ass while I sucked her left titty, grabbing the right titty. *"Lovers and Friends"* by Lil' Jon & The Eastside Boys came on and she *lost* it. She told me she had always wanted to give *me* a lap dance to that song.

The way she moved, I felt like a *nigga*–about to *bust* from the *slightest* temptation. I was *beyond* ready to sin with-and-for *Ryan*. She was *live*! I won't lie, I studied her moves. I caught myself getting jealous of the way her body moved so light, like air. Snapping out of it, realizing she was mine – *if I wanted her to be...* plus it [lap dance] was for my entertainment purposes–I was tripping... Back to enjoying her; she danced her way toward the window and let the blinds up so that the sun could shine through.

"Is you gone take that off, or do I gotta strip yo' mean, slim-thick ass?" Ryan asked.

"Come put that pussy on me." I began to take off my clothes.

"You gone let me stick my tongue in yo ass?"

(I don't like nasty shit from pretty girls, but I knew she was serious and was going to do it anyways once she went down.)

"Why you wanna be so nasty, Ry?" I asked, like I wasn't going to let her do it.

I was moving slow, fighting with my mind – I *wanted* her, but I had grown to see her as a sister, and she knew it. My shirt was off, and when I got to my pants, she stopped me and stared at the part of me that was already naked. She creeped me out. I went to grab the cover, instantly pissing her off. She threw the cover onto the floor by the closet.

She grabbed my hands, putting my arms in a triangular position–sucking my titties. She began to rub her pussy up against my knee. Turning herself on by *her own* actions, she blurted out, *"Yeah I'm bout to taste that pussy and fuck you Lissa, I'm sorry."*

Finally, she had me naked. You would have thought we were on limited time, fucking before her spouse came home (we were in my house) the way she dived in – I *liked* that shit, though. Her mouth was the *original* rose! I'm still unsure if she showed out because the blinds were open, or she felt we were *that* 'connected.' Saying that, maybe she wanted to get more 'connected.' I don't know... *I do know she had me damn near ready to tell her that I love her.*

Ryan knew what she was doing when she started this shit, there's no way in hell she didn't. After all the late nights and early mornings, she became that 'coffee' to get me through the day.

Ryan climbed on top of me, kissed me, then looked at me–more like piercing into my soul, exploring my thoughts... she was the *ultimate* adrenaline rush. She licked my lips and then bit my bottom lip... she whispered, *"I love you"* in my ear before licking and sucking them. Grabbing my neck, she kissed her way down my love trail, spelling her name with kisses and her tongue. I started to shake, normally with a female; her touch tickles me, letting me know it's not *godly*. ...Shit, a lot of things ain't godly, and with Ryan, I started to shake because I was cummin already.

Ryan caught the last drops of my juice, laughing, because the rest had already spilled onto the bed. Her hand was still on my throat, while a finger of the other hand was inside my pussy, and her thumb was rubbing my clit. Then it happened, she put them big lips on my lips and went crazy.

She went in with her tongue, matching the tempo of her finger. As pretty as she is, she had no problem getting *ugly*, *down*, and *dirty*! I made her pull out the camera – I needed to be able to witness with my eyes what she was doing to me, feeling it just wasn't enough – cause *WHAT YOU DOING??*

Finally releasing me from her grip, she opened my lips and went deeper. Pushing my legs above my head, she kissed my ass before licking my ass crack.

"Flip over," she said.

"Come eat my ass like this," I replied, while pinning my legs back.

She turned her body just enough to give me a side view. Her pussy was pretty like mine–I still didn't eat it. However, I did kiss her pussy when I brought her to me by grabbing her ass. She began to put her tongue inside my ass and for a split-second, *Jeffrey* came to mind.

So passionate... with just enough pressure. She had me inside her whirlwind, I fucking enjoyed every minute of it!

"Let me fuck that pussy," Ryan said, laughing. She laughed because the way she said it made it seem like she had a *dick*.

"Come fuck me, beautiful."

"Don't worry, I am... I just needed your permission."

With my legs *still* behind my head, she climbed on top of me, reverse-cowgirl style, and she began to rock-and-sway... the *same* way she did when she was dancing on me. She got lost in both of our juices, slipping more than she wanted. I wanted her to be in the reverse-cowgirl position in the most comfortable way possible, so I opened my legs to move them down and around her.

"Cum on this pussy," I moaned out.

"Don't tell me that. I wanna eat that pussy again."

"Come eat me up so I can cum in yo mouth."

"Yes ma'am!"

She put her hand on my stomach, to keep me from moving when I *did* start to cum. It wasn't long before she was slurping and moaning–like *she* was the one getting tongued down.

"Stop!" I screamed.

"Nope!"

I didn't have the energy to fight it anymore, she was taking *all* the life I had left... *and I let her.*

Cougar

SHIT WITH HER WAS SHORT... I was not her *speed* (and that's okay). She was *tooooooo* freaky–the 'freaky' I like in a man. I don't know what's wrong with these *nasty* ass bitches I've been meeting. This woman was *beautiful*, she worked at the local bank. She had a few streaks of grey in her hair, but nothing about her was *old*.

Her body looked amazing in *and* out of clothes. She dressed in pant suits due to her profession, but when she got out of them work clothes, she turns heads and stop cars! Right hand to God, she resembled the singer *Tweet*, she just had more ass on her. Chocolate skin, like she was cooked under the sun and kissed by the moon.

I met this woman at one of the branches on Kemp Street. I initially went in to get a new check book, but once I saw her, I was there for *her*. I knew she was *for* me the way she stared at me, she was in her glass office handling mortgages–she had no business *eyeing* me. I wasn't a thief, home buyer, nor an employee... she was just grabbing the vibe the *both* of us was putting out there.

She walked up to me in the lobby, invited me into her office, and sparked the *freakiest* conversation any strangers can exchange.

"When is the last time you had that fat, pussy sucked?" She asked.

"Girl, what the fuck wrong with you?"

"Girl!? I got a daughter your age. Stop playing before I spank yo' ass and eat that pussy."

"If there was some privacy in this muthafucka, I'd let you."

"I can get to like you."

"You don't wanna fuck with a bitch like me, besides, I'm only looking for a pet... I got too much on my plate right now."

"Oh yeah!? I just might be the person you're looking for," she replied with a smile on her face.

She didn't know, but y'all know – I love to talk freaky. We exchanged numbers; I wasn't sure if I was going to take her up on her offer, though. I wanted to fuck with her from the vibe of her not wanting to be loved... not wanting a commitment... just fun.

You would have thought I ran a sex ad, the way these bitches *flocked* to me. I didn't want another *nothing* on my plate. I was still fucking with the doctor, and *Ryan*; she replaced *Mimi*–my forever love. I never touched this woman (the bank lady), except for hugging her when we greeted one another. When fucking around, she would tie my hands just so I wouldn't touch her.

I wasn't committed to anyone, but it was a situation where I can say, *'she fucked and touched me, I didn't do shit to her.'* I wouldn't even kiss her. The months I got to know her as a human went to shit in one night when she wanted to be more than a *pet*.

Didn't Make The Cut

THIS WASN'T LOVE, BUT there were three, and I was caught up in another triangle. *Ryan*, the *doctor*, and the *cougar*. *Ryan* was someone that wasn't going away, she was there before the many bitches, *why would I let her go?* She didn't trip off of these women, but I could tell she was tired. If we're being honest, I developed a special love for her–I just didn't want a girlfriend. We were deeper than any *title*.

Ryan was more than a 'wet mouth' for me, she was *everything* I would ever want in a woman–if I see myself ever getting *serious* with a woman. Her energy shifted; it was crazy... from a mentor to a lover, to wanting to be together. The more *Ryan* and I hung out, the deeper she fell in love with every demon that lives inside of me. How would I break the news to her? This shit was deeper than *sex*... still... I wasn't with it.

Bank lady wanted me to beat her with chains, it reminded me of the time my dad asked to read my work – even though it was *erotica*. I declined his offer to read my book before publishing, and he shared that my stepmom likes to be beaten with chains. *Bank lady* also let me walk her like a dog. She was my first pet, she paid me to treat her like shit. Crazy shit... I never went overboard, but now, I was hands-on. I couldn't even choke her due to the fact that she liked to be choked until she damn near passed out. She also wanted me to spit in her mouth–I can't do no shit like that, 'I'm a laaaady' (*Sheneneh* voice).

One evening, I went to Red Lobster with her, trying to cut this shit short. But it was like once I got in front of her, it all *changed*... she *is* a *bad* ass vibe... I was just tired of juggling the three. It always starts off with an understanding – in the middle of eating my pussy and ass, then they switch up – falling in love.

I never wanted confusion from any being I fuck with. If you tell me, we're just fucking once or we're just sex partners–or anything in that form–you gotta stand on that. For the simple fact: I'll hold up *my* end of the bargain. I've never liked anyone for anything other than themselves, so it wasn't the gifts or money – hell I didn't want her. I enjoyed her soul; the shit is *beautiful*.

The *doctor* was married, I could no longer satisfy her and her husband desires. He never fucked me; he was never allowed to even ask. I enjoyed watching them fuck, but as the months went by... it got *booorrrring*. I was tired of watching–I didn't want to *join*–I was only tired of watching live porn. There was no need for me to come through once a month anymore.

I could get *Ryan* to bring in a bitch, *Jordyn* was next on the list. I felt like it was a setup, *Jordyn* hit me up herself saying she asked *Ryan* if we [Jordyn and I] could grab dinner one night, thinking *Ryan* and I were a couple. I threw *Ryan* my phone since her name was attached in the message and we were around each other at the time.

(Damn you that bold? If she were my bitch, she would have rocked her shit and I would have made sure of it.)

I told Ryan, *"If you feel disrespected, you need to check that shit... or I will."*

"Nah, I'ma watch that bitch eat you out, then I'ma make her suck my pussy before I send her home. Her approach was all wrong mama, but she bad... I won't lie." Ryan started to look for *this* 'Facebook message' *Jordyn* said she sent.

"She ain't as bad as you. It's your call, I just don't want no shit," I told her.

"You know me better than that. I ain't tripping off no bitch, I'ma need you to act like you know! I know if you weren't afraid of being in love with the same sex, I'd be for you and you know that shit too, mama."

Ryan kissed my lips and jumped on top of me. She had me out of my shell so much, I was nervous. I never wanna think in my mind that something is great, or I'm doing a great job and in reality, I suck. As she laid on top of me, I held her, I let her vent on how she wanted more.

I couldn't get past my own insecurities in order to love her or accept a being *so* beautiful would *want* to be on my arm. She was *way* prettier than I was... no need to lie.

What was I supposed to do? All these women wanted more from me... I didn't want to give it. It was hard to pick these bitches off! The *bank lady* was nothing more than a *pet* in my eyes–I had to let her go. The *nurse* and her husband had to go, too...

Ryan had to go – *back to being a friend*. I didn't give a fuck about them other bitches when it came to her, *that's my baby*. I broke my *own* heart when I broke hers. I never wanted to break her in anyway, and that's why I never wanted to cross *those lines* from the jump.

I didn't feel that I owed or that she (the bank lady) deserved an explanation, however I called her and let her know I couldn't see her anymore because I was tired of trying to manage more than one woman. Especially, when they all wanted my heart and couldn't have it. She texted and called for two weeks straight wanting to taste me. She would 'act out' to get into trouble so I could spank her–I wasn't fucking with it–the last call was her calling me a 'stupid young bitch.'

I owed *Ryan* an explanation for sure and the *nurse* deserved one (both), face-to-face.

Head Doctor

IT WAS OUR 'MONTHLY meeting day', the same day I was going to end it with her and her husband. They knew before I got there that this would be the last time. After this, they could no longer contact me, or they would be in breach of the contract established.

When I got to their house, she met me at the door with a robe on – I could tell she was horny, her nipples poked through the robe. Seeing that, I took her right titty out to get started. I wasn't in a rush, but she *looked* good in her pink robe that swept the floor. She always took advantage of looking sexy. Underneath she had on a cup-less bra with a matching thong, so I had to make her strip and dance for me.

Last time we were together, she made John wait in the room like she always did while she ate me until cum was all over her face. Tonight, we were alone.

Since this would be our last time, I told her, *"Tonight, I'll let you have your way, just don't get too crazy."*

"All I know is crazy sex, buckle up." She stripped me down out of my striped sundress.

Sucking on my neck and titties... kisses down my back as I stood in the doorway... pressing her body against mine–things got a little turned up. I let her kiss me before I pulled myself away. All I thought about was *Ryan*, I couldn't get into the kisses on my top lips [face], so I pushed her head on down to kiss me below. She got down on her knees, licking my lips before she opened me – that's when the phone rang. She didn't give a fuck she let the voicemail pick it up:

'You have reached the Chima's we're unavailable at the moment, but if you would be so kind to leave your name and a message, we will return your call at our earliest convenience. Stay forever blessed.'

(beeeeeeeeeeeep)

"Got damn, I see y'all... looks like fun. Looks like I'll be at work all night, so don't wait up for me... and don't have too much fun. Oh, and close the door before you have bugs all in the house woman," her husband said in the voicemail.

It was creepy–he was watching us–but funny for the fact that we were so into what was happening, we never noticed the door being opened.

"Let's go to the guest room for privacy," she said as she extended her hand – but I led the way. I've been all through this big muthafucka, plus I wanted to be in control tonight. Again, this was the last night and I didn't care to talk about it with her. Fuck the *'why's,'* get on this pussy!

Once we were in the guest room, I noticed it was different. They upgraded the TV to wall-size, the old one was over 70 inches (*annnnnnoooooying*). They also got the floating bed I suggested, with the clouds (cotton) and neon lights on the ceiling. I loved the mood and scenery – all that, but *Ryan* was still on the top of my brain...

This is the type of shit I wanted with *Ry* if I was going to do it. She would look like *Lucifer* under the lights. I compared her to *Lucifer* because we all know he was the most beautiful angel there was, and she has devilish ways as he did.

Jumping back into my body and out of my thoughts, I complimented her on the room, then immediately tried out the bed. As I step into the bed, I was in a bent-over position–she took it upon herself to eat my pussy from the back. I stood on the stool and arched over more so she wasn't *all* in my ass, she pulled me back down into a squat as she continued to eat my pussy.

She began to rub my pussy up-and-down, in circular motions. Then she got under and between my legs, tongue fuckin me. I got into a split while she held my back up like we were Olympic ice-skating in mid-routine.

"Yesssssss! I love the way you eat my pussy," I moaned out.

"You can have this anytime you want—but you want to end shit. My husband doesn't have to know or be involved at all."

I started to plant myself onto her face, but I didn't want to lose my balance trying to be a jackass. There was no need, anyway... she went back to sucking and fingering my pussy.

She slapped my ass, pushing me up to the bed, (I didn't expect it to be *that* sturdy). She climbed onto me from behind, giving me an Asian massage—except her services were *free*. The lights flash from pink to yellow, to lime green, to neon blue – the pattern was never the same, but it flashed off of the walls, causing me to doze off into 'La-La land.'

Ryan was on my mind, but I was no longer thinking of her. The more I laid under the light, the more I wanted peace and self-love. I didn't wanna break hearts anymore, I just happened to accidentally hurt people's feelings on purpose. I say that because shit is *preventable*, or you can cut shit short before it gets that deep.

"Hey, I think I'ma go ahead and head home. I enjoyed you over these past few months. I like you as a human and don't change who you are. Well, change that funky ass attitude," I said, while I flipped over to look her in the face.

"You don't have to end this, but I understand and won't force you. Just let me please you one last time before you go."

"Get on yo' knees and do it right." Getting on her knees like I told her... She ate my pussy better than before. I leaned down, kissed her lips for a 'job well done' and 'goodbye' before getting dressed and said my finally 'goodbye's.'

Ryan

NO MATTER HOW MUCH I thought of her, I knew I had to end it. To me, we were going nowhere and to her, we were growing as one.

Before I could sit down and talk to her, she jumped on my lap telling me about her day and how it went when she hit *Jordyn* back up.

"I feel like I'm losing you, Lissa," she said as she looked into my soul.

"You're not losing me; I just can't love you like you deserve to be loved. I never wanted this change, you did. I ain't tryna ruin your night. Finish telling me about your day."

"Business is booming. I made up a few necklaces and sold over 50 stones today. Ooooooo and back to Jordyn... she wants to know if we could have a threesome."

"You already know how I feel about a threesome–but by all means, if y'all wanna fuck around, don't let me be the reason y'all don't."

"I don't wanna fuck with her unless you're there... at least watch..."

"Love, do as you please... I ain't doing no tripping, I want you to find you somebody. If you want me there, then I'm there."

"That was extra as fuck, but okay."

She got off my lap. She wanted me to chase her, *I was not doing no shit like that.* I sat there, trying to get through to her, but nothing seemed to work – I said, 'fuck it' and grabbed my shit.

"This was your opportunity to be heard and to make sense of this... you can't make me be ready for something I'm not. Ryan I'ma only end up

hurting us both, pussy is not my main source of pleasure. I don't even fuck on you like that. I enjoy being in peace, the vibes, and how your words flow like poetry –"

She interrupted, *"It's all good. I'll hit you up when I set a date with Jordyn. You can fucking go now."*

I didn't say shit. I didn't look back. I turned the knob and put that shit in the wind. Months had gone by before she called me, telling me she thought she was ready to fuck with *Jordyn*. She wanted to know if I was available the following weekend. I told her I would come through like I promised. I didn't talk to her until the day of–she texted to see if I could still make it–I promised her I would. I told her I would still be there...

Once I got there, *Ryan* had just finished showering. To break her nervousness, she wanted to 'taste from the lake she knows is forever great!' I let her – her mouth was better than magic... she tapped into her spirit animal when she ate my pussy. I stopped her before she got too into it and delayed her dressing any longer. *Jordyn* got there and *neither* of them knew what to do.

"If me being here makes you nervous, I will leave," I said, not understanding the silence.

"No, please stay," Jordyn insisted, as she got comfortable.

"I'm only here for watching, love... I'm not the snack or dinner," I informed her.

"Well, watch this," Ryan said.

Ryan & Jordyn

RYAN and *Jordyn* began to kiss, while stripping each other, *asshole naked*. I didn't care to see them kiss, I wanted *live* porn.

"Eat her pussy and stop playing," I said, like I would if I was watching porn.

"Are you ready?" Ryan asked.

"Who you talking to…? Because I been ready. Lights, camera, action, show out!" I told Ryan, unsure of who she was initially talking to.

Jordyn never said anything, she just began walking toward the bed where I was laying. *Jordyn* was thick, but super quick. She grabbed my leg and threw them back – *Ryan* caught my legs as *Jordyn* began to eat my pussy. I didn't put up a fight, I let her bless me with her wet, beautiful mouth.

"Keep eating that pussy bitch," Ryan instructed Jordyn.

"Come join me," Jordyn replied.

Ryan got behind *Jordyn* and joined her. I started to kick both of them bitches in the face. If you've never had two mouths on you at the same time, *you're missing out*! As they ate my pussy in union, they licked each other's tongue – *now that shit was sexy…* however, I wasn't here for me.

"Get the fuck off of me!" I screamed as I released love, pain, and *recharging* energy. *Les Be Honest…* everybody ain't blessed… and I know there's no bitch blessed with this elevation I got flowing. *"Ryan, turn it upside down, mama."*

"Say less, lover," she said.

This ho' was being funny with her words, but she made *Jordyn* stand up and turn around, facing the wall with her hands on the couch.

"May I?" Ryan asked me.

"Go," I said, giving her permission to feast in front of me.

The way *Jordyn* shook and cried (literally) let me know she was just trying something. But she was barking up the wrong tree if she was thinking about me, because I don't eat *no pussy*.

Ryan wasn't eating her pussy like she did mine–not to compare–she was *into* it; she just had a lot on her mind... and I could tell.

Ryan ate *Jordyn* until she busted *three times*, back-to-back – no *Drake*.

"Before you go, bless the lady of the house and if she wants to fuck you again, she will," I told Jordyn.

I wasn't being rude, it was an 'entry' and 'exit' fee... and we only accept mouth, *sorry not sorry*. Sad to say, when this was all over, *they would never see me again.*

Jordyn

MEETING HER THROUGH *Ryan*, I never wanted to see her again. I felt like *Ryan* already snatched a piece of her soul and I wanted no parts. I was tired of these bitches *for real*. For me, sex is a way of looking deeper into another person's soul, and I don't think I wanted to go down that road again–love, heartache, and pain. I can't remember when my thoughts changed, but they did. I found myself wanting to love *Ryan*. It was something I had just realized, but after everything, I didn't want to confuse the both of us anymore than I had already did.

I didn't mean to, but I also know things change and shit happens. I honestly had no intention of getting to know *Jordyn*, but eventually, I came around. She jumped into my inbox 3 month after the whole *'Ryan and Jordyn'* thing.

She asked me if she could call me, that's when the conversation got even deeper–it felt like everything Ryan rubbed off onto her. We could relate... this woman told me her fears, dreams, goals, ups, and downs!

I felt when she talked, that she was telling her stories for the first time – I could also sense it was a weight lifted. I slowly began to fall, and this was just the *first* week. One day, I pulled up on her to talk.

** Always feeling like just a piece of meat... I figured, we could just be friends, and you know... heal one another. I wanted to cut this shit short before it got started, but I had no reason to, other than my toxic thoughts. Have you ever met someone, but you just didn't want to be involved in some bullshit–the bullshit being your own fucked up world? I wanted to spare her, as well as *Ryan* from my fucked-up past, my way of thinking, and my overall understanding.

She had been through so much. I was not about to enter her life with my wounds still open. Fast forward just a tad bit, I was searching for a way to care for her under that mucky heart and soul of hers. In searching, I learned she was honestly more than a *fine face*. She was broken, but those are the results when you love from the soul! And with her soul still being intact, she can't be *all bad*, it–just ain't no way! She's a 'bad girl' that just wants to be loved and accepted for who she is.
**

The connection and her dope conversation are what got me. She had no fears when she talked to me. Starting up (whatever we were doing), neither of us was looking for a relationship, but the shit was inevitable–like for real. I was drawn back off the top, just because of her sign (Pisces) and I swear she did everything to show me that all Pisces don't have the 'Pisces' trait.

So, you see where I'm going with it... and sex wasn't even what I was shooting for when the physical touch came back into play. I just wanted to feel her lips, her hands on me, her body heat.

Temptation is a motherfucker–I say that a lot, however, she wasn't just looking for casual sex. I also wanted to continue my celibacy journey, it secured my mind so much... but once she touched my arm, I got chills... she kissed my forehead and I melted.

With *Jordyn,* shit was different. She made me want to put the love *first*. We talked for a while and then out of the blue, I noticed her tightening her legs. She told me before I got there that she wouldn't make the first move, so it was on *me*, right?

She knew I was capable of snatching her soul, but I was not putting my mouth on her. She knew I wanted to some head, but she wanted me to ask–I just looked at her. After looking, she gave in and asked for permission to taste me. I liked that, but I didn't want to do too much, because I wasn't sure if I was going to see her again and I didn't just wanna *wild out*.

Babbbbbbby when I tell you: that young woman ate my pussy with *manners*, I mean just that! I don't even remember moving at that point. Gripping my thighs she kissed my pussy, putting her face deeper. I begged her to stop, and that's when she grabbed *both* of my wrists and ate some *more*. My legs started to shake, unable to control my own body, my left leg hit the steering wheel, causing me to press on the horn.

She got up as if she were finished, just to kiss my lips. Turning me on even *more*, I licked *me* off of her lips. I grabbed the back of her neck, shoving her face deeper than it already was, before realizing I was cumming in her mouth. I wanted another kiss after that... *Oweeeeeeee I can still feel her lips on me. (Just thinking out loud)!*

By the time she was finished, I was ready for *dick*. She motioned for me to come closer, I refused – I was ready to go now.

"Come here," she said.

"Cum where (I don't think she caught that)!?"

She looked at me like, *"you know..."* ...but I wanted her to tell me. She grabbed my arm and told me to sit on her lap. Crawling over, I sat on her lap, I was supposed to just be sitting up against her pussy, but I was so wet, we started sliding. I was mad as fuck at first because I had allowed my flesh to become so *weak* after becoming celibate. I couldn't fight it though; she pushed a finger deep inside of me... I grabbed the back of the seat to stop, and to keep myself from busting *all* over her *again*.

I started to slowly grind on her–just to make myself comfortable–and she did it again (pushed a finger *deeper* inside of me)! This time in my head I heard *D'Angelo* singing, *"Girl it's all in you, have it your way, however, you want you can decide...”* Taking control, I rode her fingers at four different speeds – while kissing her and caressing her titties. I felt her nut building up and knew it wouldn't be long before she exploded, so I fucked her finger *faster* and *harder*... before jumping off and letting her finish herself.

Tired and sweating, *Jordyn* sat back, and I laid my head on her thigh to rest. Rubbing me up and down, she started sticking her fingers inside of me, one finger at a time. At first, she sucked and licked all the juices and cream off each of her fingers. But the next time, she stuck her fingers inside me (one by one)–and one by one she stuck her fingers inside my mouth.

"Where's that butt-plug?" She whispered.

I handed it to her and went back to resting. She was gentle with the plug, but that shit hurt (she swears it's because I was super wet that it just went in, but it didn't *just* 'go in')! While laying my head on her, she began to move the plug around, in my ass. I ain't going to lie, after the plug was in, it felt *good as fuck*. I bent over so that she could kiss my ass and play with the butt plug. All the while, she *still* had a finger inside of me–I was losing all humanity... I might have sounded like a dog when I busted again.

Cussing and panting, trying to catch our breath, we looked at each other like we would be dangerous to one another.

"Man, this is not going to be the last time you fuck with me!" She blurted out. Laughing, I asked why she said that and this motherfucka said, *"Because you got some fire ass pussy, bomb ass pussy, some fire ass pussy... like no bro, you not gone just fuck me and that be it. I'm sorry, I didn't mean to call you bro... but got damn!"*

Laughing like always I told her that she'd be alright. Time started flying and I told her that I had to head home... we would see each other again, but I just wanted to be friends.

"One more time before you go?" Jordyn asked.

I let her give me the sweet lips one last time before I never saw her again. We stayed in touched, but like the others: *she/it/ they* were a phase, or entertainment for when I'm bored. I like them–male and females–then I just get tired... My mind just started going on-and-on. I thought I could talk to her about it, but she started to shut down – being confused and all.

I stopped answering the phone, I even changed one of my numbers... I just got tired of not being understood and disagreeing every time I answered the phone. Where did we go wrong? I believe it was the sex, or maybe we were never meant to fuck around.

Two months went by, and it was the same shit–but I wanted some head, so I pulled up on her again. She told me what *Ebony* told me, "*We locked in now, we fucked now we stuck.*" I wanted to say so much right then, but I didn't want to ruin the moment with my crazy ass thoughts. I wasn't into her or her feelings–I just wanted the head.

Her plan was to love one another and continue to grow individually while growing together, Like *Ryan*. Before we wrapped up the friendship, she told me, *"I got love for you, mad love... but I wanna be 'in love' with you."* With all that being done and said, we are who we are to one another. If she needs me or ever needs to talk, she knows my numbers and can hit me up on Facebook *anytime*. We didn't work–I'm the blame because she *definitely* tried. However, she said there's no love lost and no hard feelings.

I consider her to be one of my best friends, just because we both know shit about each other that we wouldn't *dare* tell another soul. We actually reconnected recently through Facebook, and she's been wanting to start over. She seems to think *she* fucked this up, but it was me... I was being *me*... I wasn't ready, I had no plans on loving her–not even a little bit. I did feel a *spark* inside me... that perhaps I *could* love a woman... not sure if it's *her*.

...Just Tired Of Both...

...Men & Women!

———

I RAN THROUGH SO MANY bitches–I feel like I can't remember their names (I'm joking). After *Mimi, Cortez, Bella, Brandy, Jordyn,* and *many* others (including *Jeffrey*), I was tired and over *all* this shit.

I no longer wanted love (if I ever *really* wanted that), I wanted *loyalty*. Love is *expensive*, and I'm not talking in the form of money. I needed a fucking breaking, literally. I was losing myself in souls that I didn't want to be attached to. I was using bitches for head and headspace – because I didn't plan on being with anyone for real. I was wasting these women's time. *I was wrong as fuck...*

Walking away from both sexes, I found peace. I could never forget the *great* girl-on-girl sex, and I could never forget the women... *karma made sure of that.*

After many years, I decided to catch up with *Ebony*, for adult conversations and shots. *Ebony* is like family, depending on my mood, I call her 'cousin.' I knew she would understand what I was going through, so catching up with her now... was perfect timing!

Ebony

EBONY... EBONY... EBONY... We've came along way from her eating my pussy in her car – and her not being able to control her emotions. Not to compare women, but she was patient like *Ryan*–except, her reason for being patient was because she was a fucking busy body. I started to say 'whore,' but that's *my lil' baby*.

When she first came at me, I thought she was playing. She was too close, like family, and she had *multiple* niggas and bitches herself. After her years of trying and me not fucking with her, she eased up on me. Now, it's been years since we've seen one another or even talked, so when she hit me up to catch up, I was game. Besides, I needed someone that understood me, my actions, and ways... a *nymphomaniac* like myself.

She hit me up around 6 PM to make sure I was still coming. I'll flake like the snow; I thoroughly enjoy being indoors, so you gotta catch me when I'm bored or already outside. I told her I was still coming and when she got off, to just hit me up. She got off early, making a liquor store run.

[Ebony] What you want from the liquor store?

[Me] Johnny Walker Black or Remy.

[Ebony] Damn, you like that strong as shit?

[Me] Yeah, that's all I drink... but if they don't have that, I'll take whiskey.

Okay, I got you. I'll text you when I get home and you can come straight over.

I didn't respond, so around 9:30, *Ebony* called me, saying,

"I'm home and I'm calling because yo ass didn't text me back."

"I was just gone wait on you to hit me when you got home. I ain't the 'bugging' type, you know that."

"Nah, yo ass be flaking. Don't play with me, bring yo ass on, I got gas money." She hung up the phone.

This is before I had my locs. However, I've always been natural, and the last time *Ebony* saw me, I had a fade with cuts in the side like the Adidas sign. I'd been in the gym working out with *Coach*, so I was well toned. Being free, I wore my hair in an afro – it was big and pretty! I had on shorts that shown that I'd been in the gym, a tank top, and sandals. I knocked on the door and heard her scream from the back that it was open, but I couldn't open it. My hands were full; I had all three phones, a bottle of water, my wallet, keys, weed, and gars. When she opened the door, she was naked. She had a hand over her pussy while her titties where exposed.

"I thought you told me you were getting in the shower, why you still naked?" I asked.

"I can't find my razor and I was straightening up. I just moved in, and I know you see these boxes everywhere. I don't need you thinking I'm nasty... yo' ass ruthless."

"Girl, shut up. I know you ain't nasty like that. You do some filthy shit but you're not dirty."

"You look good. I haven't seen you in forever."

"It's been about five years, how you been?"

"After coming home early, I decided to change my life around. I don't wanna do what I used to do. I have a real job now and I'm blessed."

I noticed her looking at me like she had something to say, so I asked her, *"Why the fuck you are looking at me like that?"*

"You so pretty to me... look at your hair, yo' body bad as fuck, and you got pretty toes."

"Don't start that shit. Hurry up and shower so we can gossip like messy bitches."

"Don't do me like that. I got this new honeypot soap; it smells so good and it's black owned. Okay I'm bout to get my fat ass in the shower."

I sat there on the couch texting *Chevy*, tryna help him through his situation. I loved him and understood the fact that he loved me and another woman – I wasn't first in the picture, so I wasn't hurt by it either. I always told him that I fucked with a bitch, but I don't ever think he believed that I fucked with one while falling in love with him. He had a girlfriend at the time, so me fucking with someone wouldn't have been an issue to me – but for him, he was against it. He didn't want me fucking with a bitch unless he could fuck her too... he even let me know that *his* bitch *also* liked bitches, and we could all fuck around until he got her off his plate.

I said all that because *that* came up in the conversation we had on the phone while *Ebony* was in the shower. I wasn't even tryna go there at that woman's house, speaking on conversations we usually had when no one was around. We cut the conversation short at the same time–his bitch came outside looking for him and *Ebony* was getting out the shower.

"Here comes this nosey bitch. I love you, Lissa; I know I got a lot on my plate and once I get it right, I want to be with you," Chevy said.

"I love you too. I hate the situation; you know I never wanted this for us. I ain't asking you to leave her, it's not your fault that I just so happened to fall in love."

"That's the thing Lissa, this shit ain't one sided."

"Hey, this ain't the time... forever locked in. Don't crash out is all that I ask."

"I'm about to crash out, I can feel it. That's why I went to talk to my son. Just know whatever happens, I really do love you. If shit were my way, I'd be up under you right now."

"We can't always have what we want, but I do love you, and I'm not tripping on a bitch that was here before me. I think she's pretty and you fuck up too much, that's her reason for fighting on you. This shit we got going can't be hidden, so clean it up–I'll be here. 'Friends first,' I always said that, and I mean that. I feel there's nothing we can't come back from. You got a whole baby on the way and it's not by her, bro... tighten up, please. I love you, go make that shit work and get it right. Stop hiding outside and go inside and talk to her, that's a part of adulting and communicating."

"I know, but you are the only person that understands me. Just know I love you. I'll call you in the morning."

"I love you too, Chevo... call me when you wake up. My ringer is on... and get some rest, too... rest your body."

"Alright, I love you again... just know. Bye, baby."

"You didn't have to hang up because I'm out the shower," Ebony said to me.

"O nah, I got off the phone because the conversation was over. Shut the fuck up and don't start with me."

"Let's take a shot. I don't drink like I used to, but I'll take a few shots with you."

"I'm bout to roll up, I ain't bout to be in here drunk with yo' freaky ass."

"I'm not tryna get you drunk, cousin–I just want to have some fun, catch up... and I'm not getting high with you–you smoke too much."

She poured us both a double shot before going to put some clothes on. When she came out of her room, she had on a gray short-set, no bra–but she had panties on. She looked so healthy. She still smoked cigarettes (not around me), but she wasn't popping pills. I was happy for her glowing, hair growing, and not so full of emotions.

"Lissa, you got thick, what the fuck you been doing?" Ebony asked.

"Writing and dancing –" I said before she interrupted me.

"– I know bitch, stop fucking dancing! I'm tired of my man waking up excited to see you dance at five in the fucking morning! That shit is sexy, though... I never knew you could dance."

"I really be nervous to post that shit. I just love to escape, and women encourage me to post dance videos to give them motivation in the bedroom."

"Come dance for me. I'll put on some music," she said. She went to turn on some music, I can't remember the song, however the beat is still in my head. Watching her backside view, I heard *Chevy* voice saying, *"You should..."* He always said that when I said I didn't eat pussy. I tried it before, and it was nasty! Not nasty but *masty*! She (the bitch I tried it on) wrong as hell – deadly silent killer she has got in between her legs. So, it was damn near nine years since I tried it again. Kissing *Ryan's* pussy doesn't count.

I don't know *what* the fuck got into me... I started having these thoughts, *needing* what my mind was *feeding* me. She bent over like she felt me staring at her ass. I wanted to get up and rub on that *big* ass, but I told myself that's not what I was there for... but I think it really *was*. We catch up when we link, but she eats my pussy as well. She danced to the music until she found a song. She wanted me to dance, too, however I wasn't dancing. She was the ex-stripper, I wanted *her* to dance for *me*.

"Come here," I said.

"Dance for me."

"Nah. You dance for me... come here."

She got into my lap like I was paying her. She threw it back, slowly grinding as I grinded back. I wasn't going to dance *for* her, but I was willing to dance *with* her. She reached down and rubbed on my pussy, turning me on even more... I rubbed her pussy with my left hand, while I gripped her big soft ass with my right hand.

"You got me dancing and you supposed to be dancing for me," she said. I told her to shut up and pushed her hand down to her feet. In doing that, she began to bounce her ass up-and-down, as if she were riding dick. She leaned over to the end table to pour us a shot. I told her to get off me because I was *horny*. She laughed, letting me know she could take care of *that* if I wanted her to. I told *Ebony* that I wasn't going to get drunk – but here I was... ready to do *whatever*. She went to change the music to something slower, changing the mood. I came up from behind and began to kiss the back of her thighs, opening her legs so I could kiss her pussy.

"No, stop! I'm a bottom, I don't want you to do anything to me... let me please you. You are scaring me, you ain't never acted gay, you tryna turn me out," Ebony said.

"Bitch please! You know I don't like pussy like that."

"But I do... get naked."

"I ain't getting naked for you, but I'll take off my shorts."

Ebony wasn't going for that; she began to pull on my clothes as if they should *tear* when pulled. She poured us up another double shot, while I sparked up the blunt. I was three puffs in when I tried to pass *Ebony* the blunt, but she moved my hand and grabbed my legs.

"I been waiting years to eat this pussy again," She said.

"Stop all that talking and go for what you know."

The way her mouth *violated* my pussy on the *first* lick drove me *insane*! That bitch's tongue is like a tornado–I would say she's the best pussy eater out of them all... *but...* I'ma need to feel the *other* woman's mouth to remember.

She is the *pussy beast*–fuck the *pussy monster*! I was so inebriated, I thought she was eating me whole. I was cool with it – bitch swallowed me whole, having mixed feelings like *Job* inside the belly of the whale. I wanted to cry, scream, and shout. She didn't have to do too much for me to cum, I done that *twice* before the orgasm. I thought about letting *Chevy* fuck her, but I didn't want her to think she could fuck me *with her man*.

I was thinking about *Chevy*... it felt like cheating, only because he has my heart. In the mist of me being in deep thought, her nigga started calling. We were drunk, so when he called, she would answer, laugh, and tell him she was with her cousin, having 'girl's night,' then hang up. She did that–man, like five times–before I heard him shout, *"You gay ass bitch, you probably over there eating pussy,"* through the phone. She hung up the phone and he left a voice clip saying how he was going to come kick down her door.

"Girl I'm about to go, y'all too crazy for me! You ain't bout to get me beat up with you. Fuck that," I said.

"I'm not worried about that nigga, lay back down and let me finish eating that pussy."

"Nah... you lay back and let me eat yo pussy."

"I don't let females give me head."

"I just wanna try it. Trust me I'm not tryna suck on you til you cum, I just want to taste you."

"Lissa, you are scaring me."

"Bitch lay back!" I demanded.

She didn't fuss... she laid back, prepping for what *could* be the absolute *worst* head of her life – or basic head, because I was nowhere *near* a 'pro.' I started to lick her pussy and she moaned and grabbed my hair. Turning her on *turned me on,* so I began to suck her pussy. I was drunk as fuck, so I didn't notice how hard I was sucking her pussy until she told me she doesn't like her pussy to be sucked like *that. Ebony* coached me through it, and I'm kind of embarrassed to say–I liked it. I wanted to eat her pussy again–not *that same* night... but eventually.

She was shocked... *so was I*, but that wasn't enough for her. She wanted to continue eating my pussy... and she did. The shots finally caught up to me, I pushed her off of me because I felt myself getting ready to throw up.

"Bitch you better not throw up on my rug," Ebony said as she pushed me towards the bathroom.

"I'm not. Open the door so I can throw up... and call me a Lyft."

"Here, drink this water... I'm not drinking with you no more."

"Man, shut the fuck up and open the door!"

"Just throw up in that box and set it outside."

I ended up throwing up in the box, I sat it outside and then told her the code to my phone in order to get me a Lyft.

She said, *"Drink that water and come lay down..."* That's all I remember...

I woke up the next morning on the couch feeling gay as fuck, tired, and *still horny*. She woke up once she felt my movement, grabbing onto me tighter like we were lovers. I reached over her for my phone, waking her up, completely. She told me how drunk I was and began eating my pussy. I texted the Lyft driver as soon as I grabbed my phone. I lowkey hate that I did, she was eating like it was the *last supper*! I got a text saying my Lyft was five minutes away, so I got up to get dressed while she laid there playing in her pussy with a dildo.

"Why you getting dressed?" She asked.

"I wasn't even supposed to be here this long, but I'ma grab that box and take it before I go."

"What's wrong? Why you leaving?" She questioned me, like she was *my woman.*

Nothing was wrong. I overstayed my welcome, and she wasn't my bitch. She looked at me with so much disappointment, but I couldn't do it. I wanted to clear my head and talk, not cloud my mind anymore. We did neither, I know I sound ungrateful, but she gives me *bad vibes* and bad luck. She swears we're forever locked in; I believe her, but for some reason, we clash like lovers and I'm *tired* of cussing her stupid ass out.

Year Later... The Rundown

———

I NEVER THOUGHT I WOULD cross paths with most of these women after the way I just dropped them. Thank God for maturity and growth... on both ends. It boggles my mind the way social media works... That's how we all got reconnected!

Nyla – I hadn't talked to her since high school, I always thought about her. Not even on no 'fuck' shit, I just wondered if she was okay. It was like one day, she just up and disappeared off of the map. Her profile popped up on my Facebook, so I shot her a friend request and we caught up. I even talked to her about *Mimi*. She popped back up on some 'love' shit, and *Nyla* was giving me advice – only to turn around to tell me she was being *sarcastic*. I told her about this book (*Les Be HONEST*) and she asked to read her part. She laughed at me, acting like she never knew I liked her like *that*.

DeDe – We reconnected on Facebook. I feel so bad for the way I treated her. I just wasn't ready. I thank God for her, she's an *amazing* woman. I'm proud of her, she has many degrees under her belt and is *glowing* more than ever! We've reached a point to where we can talk about the past and our current love life.

She's also one of my *biggest* supporters in my life of writing. I'm glad we can still be friends after all the pain I caused.

Mimi – After *Nyla* told me to give *Mimi* a chance, I did... It was a slap in the face; this bitch tried to play me. This bitch started texting me saying she *'love me still'* and a whole 'lotta other bullshit.

She told me her kids needed food and she was still without power after the snowstorm cleared. I was in the hospital recovering from surgery–I didn't wanna talk–I asked her how much she need.

She started acting dumb! I sent $50 to her phone so she could pick it up from Walmart. This bitch called talking about *WE* can't get it to work, and that they needed a pin number. I send her goofy ass everything that she needed to get the change, and she never picked it up!

A day later, she was on Facebook saying how her nigga dick was little. She *weird as fuck*, and I hate that I listened to *Nyla*, cause that hoe trash. I was *iffy* about talking to her anyways because she has 5 kids now, wanting to be a family... no ma'am! You need you a nigga!

Cortez, Bella, and Brandy – I don't fuck with *either* of these muthafucka! *Cortez* can't stop her brother from liking me, so she won't even speak. *Bella* hit me up one day about writing and she pissed me off, so I blocked her from my Facebook. All she said was, *"Soooooo... I think I'm ready to try this writing thing."* She shouldn't have called writing a 'thing!' *Brandy*... Lord, I hope I *never* see her big ol' fat ass!

Ryan – I ran across her on Facebook, but I didn't want to disturb her peace. I looked at a few of her pictures and kept it moving, forever wishing the best for her. She's in a relationship with her best friend. He sent me a friend request, asking me to check out his music. In his video, I saw this light chick that looked exactly like *Ryan*, it *was* her. She does these events in Dallas where she reads cards and promotes everything *spiritual*.

Doctor – She sent me a friend request–I didn't accept it. I just didn't want to be bothered. I know she's divorced now, *and that ain't my problem.*

Bank Lady – This hoe was *crazy*; she reminds me of *Brandi*, from *Its A Thin Line Between Love & Hate*. Neeeeext!

Jordyn – She hit me up as I was reading through this book wanting to 'fix us.' I just told her flat out, *"I'm not going backwards."* We can be friends, but that 'love, relationship, sex-slave' shit is dead... I want P E A C E, got damn me.

Ebony – She rides for me so tough, it's hard for me to believe it! *Ebony* has always done too much, that shit stems from her traumatic ass childhood. She's not my bitch, but she is loyal.

The End